THE GIGANTIC SHADOW

Bill Hunter, TV personality, made his living by asking the rich and famous difficult and highly personal questions, but when the tables were turned and he found himself being asked about his own rather murky past, he wasn't quite so sure of himself. Out of a job and with little hope of finding another, he teamed up with the reckless Anthea to embark upon a dangerous and deadly plan that was to have murderous consequences.

THE GIGANTIC SHADOW

by

Julian Symons

Dales Large Print Books
Long Preston, North Yorkshire,
BD23 4ND, England.

British Library Cataloguing in Publication Data.

Symons, Julian
The gigantic shadow.

A catalogue record of this book is available from the British Library

ISBN 1-84262-371-0 pbk

Cover illustration by arrangement with House of Stratus

Published in Large Print 2005 by arrangement with House of Stratus

Dales Large Print is an imprint of Library Magna Books Ltd.

Printed and bound in Great Britain by
T.J. (International) Ltd., Cornwall, PL28 8RW

INTRODUCTION

The French call a typewriter *une machine á ècrire*. It is a description that could well be applied to Julian Symons, except the writing he produced had nothing about it smelling of the mechanical. The greater part of his life was devoted to putting pen to paper. Appearing in 1938, his first book was a volume of poetry, *Confusions About* X. In 1996, after his death, there came his final crime novel, *A Sort of Virtue* (written even though he knew he was under sentence from an inoperable cancer) beautifully embodying the painful come-by lesson that it is possible to achieve at least a degree of good in life.

His crime fiction put him most noticeably into the public eye, but he wrote in many forms: biographies, a memorable piece of autobiography (*Notes from Another Country*), poetry, social history, literary criticism coupled with year-on-year reviewing and two volumes of military history, and one string thread runs through it all. Everywhere there is a hatred of hypocrisy, hatred even when it aroused the delighted fascination with which he chronicled the siren schemes of that notorious jingoist swindler, Horatio Bottomley, both in his biography of the man and fictionally in *The Paper Chase* and *The Killing of Francie Lake*.

That hatred, however, was not a spew but a well-spring. It lay behind what he wrote and gave it force, yet it was always tempered by a need to speak the truth. Whether he was writing about people as fiction or as fact, if he had a low opinion of them he simply told the truth as he saw it, no more and no less.

This adherence to truth fills his novels with images of the mask. Often it is the mask of hypocrisy. When, as in *Death's Darkest Face* or *Something Like a Love Affair*, he chose to use a plot of dazzling legerdemain, the masks of cunning are startlingly ripped away.

The masks he ripped off most effectively were perhaps those which people put on their true faces when sex was in the air or under the exterior. 'Lift the stone, and sex crawls out from under,' says a character in that relentless hunt for truth, *The Progress of a Crime*, a book that achieved the rare feat for a British author, winning Symons the US Edgar Allen Poe Award.

Julian was indeed something of a pioneer in the fifties and sixties bringing into the almost sexless world of the detective story the truths of sexual situations. 'To exclude realism of description and language from the crime novel' he writes in *Critical Occasions*, 'is almost to prevent its practitioners from attempting any serious work.' And then the need to unmask deep-hidden secrecies of every sort was almost as necessary at the end of his crime-writing life as it had been at the beginning. Not for nothing was his last book subtitled *A Political Thriller*.

HRF Keating
London, 2001

Again, for Kathleen

Chapter One

'The name's Mekles,' Jerry Wilton said. 'Nicholas Mekles. You must have heard of him.'

Should he have suspected something then, should there have been some small jarring shudder, like the moment when the fated ship first noses into the iceberg? Such a premonition would have been irrational, and Hunter liked to think that his life was ruled by reason. He felt nothing.

'The name is familiar,' he said. 'But the fame escapes me.'

Jerry wiped his red face with a grey silk handkerchief. It was a hot day in early June, and the window in his small office was closed.

'I don't know what you read, but it isn't the papers,' he grumbled. 'Mekles is always in the news. Big parties on his yacht, the *Minerva*, in the Med. or the Adriatic. Film actress fell off it during one of them, got herself drowned, she was his mistress, people said she might have been pushed. Owns a shipping fleet, shady goings-on I seem to remember in relation to that, Charlie Cash can dig it out for you. Gambles a lot, Monte

Carlo, Nice. Fabulous villa out there on the Riviera, more big parties, socialites rubbing shoulders with crooks. Never married, but women queue up for him, socialites again a lot of them. And more, lots of it, the same sort. Plenty for Charlie to get his teeth into.'

'I remember him now,' Hunter said. 'A sort of blend of playboy and gangster.'

'More gangster than playboy. There are all sorts of rumours about him. They say he keeps half a dozen thugs as bodyguards. Also that he takes a lot of trouble to get the dirt on anyone he has dealings with.' Jerry looked at the three pills on his desk, blue, green and white, selected the blue one, popped it in his mouth and swallowed.

Even then Hunter felt no anticipatory tremor. 'A pretty tough customer.'

Jerry nodded solemnly. His face was glistening again, but this time he did not bother to wipe it. 'He's coming to England on Friday week, staying over till Tuesday. We've approached him, told him about the programme, and he's agreed in principle.'

'Why would a man like that want to go in front of the cameras?' Hunter wondered. 'He's got a lot to hide.'

'Vain as a peacock. Likes to show off in front of his women. Tickled to death to be asked.'

'Even on my programme?'

'Especially on your programme. Nicholas

Mekles pitting his wits against those of TV's special investigator and coming out on top – what a thrill for him. And anyway, it's fame to be on that little old silver screen, something money can't buy. Don't tell me I've got to teach you psychology as well as fixing the programmes,' Jerry cried in a pretended exasperation that only just missed being real. Hunter watched, fascinated, as he picked up the green pill and swallowed it, as he had the blue, without water. 'Replaces the salt you lose through sweat,' Jerry explained. 'Salt makes energy. You take three in half an hour, twice a day. They cost thirty bob a packet. What do you think?'

'It seems all right.' He had found in the past that it was never wise to show too much enthusiasm.

'All right!' Jerry flung up his hands. 'I serve up something like this on a plate for you, something that's really the chance of a lifetime to turn a gangster inside out, and you say it seems all right.' Again there was an undercurrent of real annoyance beneath the jocularity.

'When I say all right, I mean I like it.' And he did mean it, he had no real reservations. 'It seems to me we've got to be a bit cagey, that's all. The thing's got slander possibilities sticking out all over it.'

'Just a matter of the way you handle it.' With agreement obtained, Jerry was mellow, calmly judicial.

'Make the questions too soft and we get nowhere. Make them too hard, and we get a slander action up our shirts.'

'I don't think Mekles can afford to bring slander actions. Anyway you can handle it, you and Charlie, you've handled trickier ones.' Jerry exuded confidence, went so far as to give a wink from the little blue eye in his boiled red face. 'After all, it's the trickiness that makes the programme, isn't that right? Now, let's get down to brass tacks.'

Before Hunter left, Jerry had swallowed the white pill.

Chapter Two

Hunter's television programme was called 'Bill Hunter – Personal Investigator', and it had a subsidiary heading tacked on: 'Presents the News Behind the News.' The programme ran for a quarter of an hour each week, and consisted simply of an unscripted interview with some celebrated or notorious person. There were, however, unusual features about it. Most programmes billed as 'unscripted' are so only in name – the protagonists have discussed very thoroughly in advance the course that the programme is to take.

Hunter, however, had stipulated from the start that he should not meet his subject in advance, or discuss a line of questioning with him. The questions might be disconcerting, the answers might come as a surprise to Hunter. The programme therefore rightly appeared to viewers as a battle of wits.

This impression was enhanced by the fact that the people interviewed had always a slightly gamey flavour about them. They were film stars famous for the number or nature of their love affairs, generals suddenly sacked or demoted, extreme Left or Right wing politicians, surprisingly rich American trade unionists, organisers of nudist colonies, former members of secret societies devoted to violence. To the watchers sitting comfortably in their armchairs it seemed that the people interviewed were being ruthlessly quizzed by a Personal Investigator who had discovered a complete range of skeletons in their cupboards.

In fact, the questions were all based upon the material unearthed by Hunter's research assistant Charlie Cash, and Charlie's research rarely went beyond industrious digging in old newspaper cuttings plus the fruits of intelligent guesswork from conversations with friends around Fleet Street. Occasionally questions based on Charlie's speculations provoked unexpected reactions, and the person interviewed got really annoyed.

These were the moments when the watchers in suburban semis wriggled most deliciously in their overstuffed armchairs, the moments that fixed the Personal Investigator in their minds as an inquisitorial father figure extracting secrets from mentally-tortured victims. The idea was seven-eighths illusion, but then, as Hunter sometimes reflected, wasn't the whole apparatus and effect of TV designed to create an illusion? The difference between TV and the cinema, he had once heard someone say, was that while both created legendary figures, the cinema did not try to deny that they were fabulous while TV pretended that they were just homebodies like you and me.

Reality faced him now, however, reality quite undeniable, in the shape of Charlie Cash sitting across the table from him in Charlie's little Fleet Street office, a dusty cubicle filled with law and reference books, quite remote from Jerry Wilton's splendour of glass walls and chromium fittings. Charlie sat behind a table spilling over with papers. He had a long thin nose, sloping shoulders, and the hungry look of a good research man. He twisted a toothpick in his mouth.

'Here's the stuff on Nick the Greek.' He handed over two large envelopes marked A and B. The first contained facts, the second what Charlie called his intelligent guess-work. There would be a separate page for each story, and appended to the story would be a note from Charlie about its origins and possible use. Charlie, with the aid of a secretary, gave this kind of service to a dozen people, and got well paid for it.

'Is he a Greek?'

'He's rich, a crook, a commercial genius. Must be a Greek or an Armenian or a Jew, isn't that right, statistics can't lie. Anyway they say he carries a Greek passport, though there seems to be a bit of mystery about it.'

'How does it strike you?'

Charlie looked down his long nose. 'Not too good.'

'Jerry thought we were on to a winner.'

'Jerry believes what he reads in the papers. He doesn't know a tiger from pussy. This Mekles is a nasty piece of work.'

'We've handled nasty pieces of work before now.'

'Yes, but this is different. The stuff about our friend Nick that Jerry is thinking of is really old hat. That girl who fell off the yacht, for instance, Lindy Powers–'

'The film actress?'

'That's what they called her. She had a bit part in a B film, then lay around Hollywood until Mekles picked her up. Anyway, the press did that to death at the time. If you want to give it another going over, you can, but it's stale stuff. Same with a lot of the rest of it. There was a story that he had some famous stolen paintings in his villa on the Riviera. Mekles showed reporters round, turned out the paintings had been bought through art dealers, only he'd bought shrewdly and cheaply. That sort of thing.'

'Do you mean we haven't got a story?'

'You've got a story, only I don't see how you're going to tell it without landing up to your neck in slander. And other trouble too, I dare say. Nasty revengeful type friend Nick is said to be.'

'What's the story, then?'

'There are half a dozen, and they're all poison. You know the international groups controlling tarts are supposed to have taken a knock since the Messina brothers were put inside? So that the import of French tarts into Britain by marriages of convenience almost stopped, for instance? Well, in the last few months the organisation has got a lot tighter again. Mekles is said to be one of two or three people controlling it. Then drugs – he's said to have both the import-export and the distribution ends tied up. It's distribution that's the problem as you know, getting the stuff into and out of the country is easy here, not like the States. Fake antiques is another sideline – there's still a ready sale for them in the States, though Americans have smartened up a lot in the last few years and look twice at worm holes made with a drill. But Mekles has an east end factory turning out the stuff.'

'Let's get down to cases, Charlie. How much of this can I use?'

Charlie dropped the toothpick into a waste basket, picked another. 'I thought I'd made that plain. None of it.'

'None of it?'

'I don't see how you can. It's all B stuff. I know it, but there's no proof. Take the factory. It runs as a perfectly straight concern, making cheap furniture that falls to bits when you use it. Now, a pal of mine named Jack Foldol, a bookie's tout, knows the manager at this factory, a White Pole, if you know what I mean, named Kosinsky. One day Kosinsky told him about the other stuff they made, and the prices they got for it. Kosinsky also said that one day Myerson, that's the man who's supposed to own the place, had made a terrific fuss about an important conference, cleared everyone out of the place. Kosinsky was curious, managed to hang around, saw Mekles arrive, recognised him from newspaper photographs. Kosinsky hasn't any doubt it was Mekles, heard a little bit of what they were saying, enough to know that Mekles was giving Myerson orders.'

'If it was Mekles.'

'That's what I mean. It's all hearsay stuff. I told you you couldn't use it.'

'Does Mekles come here often? From the

way Jerry spoke I thought this was a first visit.'

'Hell, no, he's been in England a dozen times. Why should they keep him out, he's a solid citizen. It's a headache, and I'm glad it's yours.'

Hunter nodded, took the envelopes. He had, even now, no warning presentiment. He had made good programmes out of less promising material.

'How's Anna?' It was a question Charlie never forgot to ask. 'That's a great little woman, Bill. One of these days I'm going to come along and take her away from you. In the meantime, don't forget to kiss her foot for me, will you?'

Chapter Three

On that Monday night he stepped into the hotel's revolving door, was whirled round, and then whirled round again before he got out. Inside he spoke to a commissionaire. 'Mekles,' he said, 'Mr Nicholas Mekles.'

On the commissionaire's face there was a fine glaze of disapproval. 'Mr Mekles is on the fourth floor, sir.'

Are your eyes fixed so that you can't look at me when you speak? he wanted to ask.

But before he could say anything a voice called from the other side of the reception hall and he saw Jerry Wilton, sweating and anxious.

'Been looking out for you, Bill. How are you?'

'How should I be? Hot.' Outside the night was hot, in here it was cool, but the air conditioning had a stifling effect. He wanted to pull his shirt collar open.

'We're all set. Less than quarter of an hour to spare.' Jerry managed to sound reproachful. 'I've been talking to Mekles. He seems a nice little chap, most co-operative. Just time for a word with him, if you'd like one.'

'No, thanks.' Jerry always wanted him to talk to the subjects, and he always refused. 'I'd like a drink.'

'A drink, yes, of course.' Jerry's anxiety was perceptibly increased, but he was brave about it. 'There's a bar round to the left. Let's make it a quick one, you know me, just a time slave, like to be on the platform half an hour before the train goes.'

While they drank whisky Jerry turned round a ring on his finger, tapped the counter, scratched one leg with the other, did everything but look at his watch. 'How did the programme come along?'

'Terrible. Just terrible!'

'What's that?' Jerry looked as though he had heard a priest reading from a handbook on atheism.

'I told you, terrible. We like to play with squibs and you've given me a stick of dynamite. You'd better hope I won't set a match to it.' He held out his glass for another whisky.

Jerry stared, then laughed. 'You aren't serious, Bill.'

'Perfectly serious.' What makes me needle him, Hunter wondered, even though the needling is the truth, and it probably will be a terrible programme.

When they got out of the lift at the fourth floor flexes were trailing all over the place. Two electricians were hanging about, and there was a stocky man with a cauliflower ear in the corridor.

'One of Mekles' bodyguards,' Jerry whispered. 'He really does have them. And do you know, Bill, he's taken the whole bloody floor? What it is to be rich, eh?' Admiration was blended with envy in Jerry's voice.

'What it is to come out on top in the rat race.'

Jerry looked at him, said nothing. They turned left into the room where the telecast was to take place, and Hunter walked under the intense heat of the arcs. Three or four people began talking to him at once. Would he sit down in his special chair, raise his head, raise his hand, lean forward. He did all that. While the make-up men were working on his face, brushing his jacket, he saw Charlie Cash hovering in the background, and raised a hand.

Charlie came over. 'You've got everything?'

'In here.' Hunter tapped his head.

'Got a line to work on?'

'I put my trust in God.'

'You believers.' Charlie turned down the corners of his mobile comedian's mouth, went away.

Jerry Wilton walked over to an inner room, opened the door, spoke to somebody there, came back.

'We're on in one minute. Quiet, please.'

There was silence. Hunter could feel sweat trickling down the back of his neck. He wanted to wipe his forehead, but didn't dare to do so. The green light showed and he heard a voice full of synthetic excitement and enthusiasm saying:

'And now we bring you again our News Behind the News programme, with Personal Investigator Bill Hunter in another candid, unscripted, no-holds-barred interview with one of the most interesting personalities in London this week, with–'

Now on more than a million television screens the announcer's face was replaced by Hunter's, and he began to talk: '–a modern mystery man, Mr Nicholas Mekles. To many of us Mr Mekles is a name. We know of him as the owner of a shipping fleet. He is lucky enough to have a fabulous villa on the Riviera and an equally fabulous yacht. He is reputed to exercise control over a dozen different organisations. Some people say he is the richest man in the world.' Hunter paused, so that his next words should take on an emphasis that was not in his voice. 'How has Mr Mekles reached his present position? Where did the money come from? Those are two of the intriguing questions I propose to ask this man of mystery. Mr Mekles is paying one of his occasional visits to London – he has taken the whole fourth floor of the Park Lane Grand Hotel, and it's from a room in his suite that I am talking to you. And now, let's meet the man of mystery.'

The cameras followed him as he walked across the room and tapped on the inner door. This door opened and Mekles came out, a man like a very elegant lizard, olive-skinned and sweetly smiling, with small snapping dark eyes.

The two men sat down, Hunter with his back to the cameras so that the audience looked past him at Mekles. For the rest of the programme the watchers would never see Hunter's face. The effect had been adapted from an American programme, to give the impression of a man being judged rather than questioned. The cameras shifted occasionally to give a glimpse of Hunter's shoulder as they looked over it, or to show the back of his head. Mekles, beyond him and in a lower chair, looked like a criminal undergoing interrogation.

Open mildly. 'Can you tell me, Mr Mekles, how this man-of-mystery label got attached to you?'

The little man in the chair below him shrugged. His tongue shot out, briefly licked narrow lips. His voice was low, musical, the words perfectly comprehensible but the stress on syllables foreign. 'I am a businessman. What is there mysterious about that? This man of mystery, you know, I think he does not exist. He has been invented by newspaper reporters looking for a story.' His smile broadened. 'Perhaps by television interviewers too.'

The victim should not answer back. Hunter said sharply, 'A businessman. What kind of business?'

'Any kind that is offered. I buy things cheap, I sell them at a profit. That kind of business.'

'Three years ago your name was mentioned in connection with an international report into the control of prostitution in Europe, and the shifting of prostitutes from one country to another.' Mimicking Mekles' accent slightly, Hunter asked, 'That kind of business?'

It was his belief that the only way in which

the interview could take on some sort of life was by his angering Mekles. To his disappointment the little man seemed unmoved. He said carefully, 'As you know, I am sure, I was cleared of any suggestion that I had any connection with such horrible traffic.'

'You own a shipping fleet?' Mekles inclined his head. 'Is it a fact that several ships of that fleet sank with valuable cargo on board?'

'Four ships only.'

'And that the insurance companies concerned refused to pay on the ground that the ships were not seaworthy?'

No feeling of any sort showed in the little dark eyes. 'Not at all. One of the insurance companies paid without question. The other refused to pay, on what I could only regard as a pretext. I took the only step available to me.'

Incautiously Hunter asked, 'What was that?'

'I bought the insurance company.' Without raising his voice Mekles said, 'I am quite a respectable man, I assure you, Mr Hunter. As respectable as you are, perhaps. I have big oil interests, I own a great deal of property, some of it in England. Would you like me to tell you about that?'

The interview was going badly, creating the wrong impression. It was almost as though Mekles were the interrogator and

Hunter the man under questioning. And it was hot, too hot under the arc lamps. Hunter felt the heat striking at him, soaking his shirt, making his collar limp, beating at his eyes and forehead, as he went on asking questions, making wild roundhouse verbal swings which Mekles parried with almost contemptuous ease, saying that there was no mystery about his passport, it had been issued by the Greek Government, there was no mystery about his origin, he was a Greek citizen, he had come to England merely for pleasure. 'It is a very nice country,' he said. 'Your policemen are wonderful. Also your television interviewers.'

Hunter discovered in himself a dislike, almost hatred, for the little man sitting opposite him. He remembered suddenly a note made by Charlie Cash. 'Mekles is supposed to be here to get in touch with Melville Bond, ex-MP, businessman, director Bellwinder Tool Co. Some sort of shady deal proposed, Mekles boss, Bond carrying out instructions. Like the furniture factory I told you about.' Underneath came Charlie's comment: 'Unconfirmed. Don't know what it's all about. Just info., not to use.'

Sometimes a shot in the dark could be successful. It had happened before, it could happen again. He said, 'So you are here purely for pleasure?'

'Purely. I find all sorts of things pleasant.

Even an interview like this one when I am being – what do you call it? – grilled.'

'Business absolutely doesn't enter into it?'

Sharply Mekles said, 'It does not.'

Hunter leaned forward. The camera, looking down, showed his broad shoulders, the back of his head. 'Do you know a man named Melville Bond?'

There was a flicker of hesitation, no more. 'No.'

'You haven't been in touch with him?'

'Not at all.'

'You have done no business with him?'

'None whatever.'

There was something here. Hunter could feel it. He said encouragingly, 'Perhaps you used another name for the purpose? Or approached him through an agent? In an important business deal you might well not wish to appear personally.'

'I have no knowledge whatever of Mr Bond.' Mekles drew back in the chair, put out his tongue again, and Hunter was suddenly aware of danger, of a transformation from lizard to snake. 'And on the question of using false names you have personal knowledge, I think.'

The attack was so sudden that Hunter was jolted by it, committed again the mistake of allowing Mekles the initiative. 'What do you mean?'

'I mean that your name is not Hunter but

O'Brien. You have spent several years in prison for a crime which I will be friendly enough not to name. I cannot admit that you have any right to ask me such questions as you have done. I must ask you to excuse me.'

All this the viewers in suburban semis delightedly heard and saw; saw, too, the bulk of the interviewer as Hunter stepped down from his chair and moved towards Mekles, arms swinging. Then the transmission was cut off and replaced by an urbane announcer, apologising.

In the room, Hunter barely grazed Mekles' jaw with a right swing. He heard Jerry and Charlie Cash both crying out, and turned just in time to take a blow on the side of the face from the man with the cauliflower ear. He slipped sideways, tripped over one of the trailing wires, was conscious of thunderous bangs and crashes all about him, and then knew nothing more.

Chapter Four

Two people bent over, smiling at him. The smiles on their faces were upside down. His head ached. He put up a hand to it, and felt bandages. He closed his eyes and opened them again and the people were right way up, Charlie Cash and Anna. He was lying on the sofa in the living room of the flat which he shared with Anna. With that fact established, he closed his eyes again.

Anna's voice, soft as melted toffee, said, 'Bill, darling, are you awake?'

Charlie's sharp Cockney voice said, 'You've got those bandages on because you tripped and brought one of the cameras down on the side of your head. No serious damage. If you can open your eyes and talk, you'd better.'

It was Charlie's voice he answered, opening his eyes. Anna knelt by the sofa, her soft pudgy face inches from his. 'Are you sure you can talk?'

'I can talk.' He swung his legs to the ground and groaned at the pain in his head. 'Tell me what happened.'

'The interview was rotten. Then you asked some questions about Bond. Mekles came back with some stuff about your name being O'Brien. You took a poke at him.' Charlie paused. With no change of tone he added, 'That all went out. Anna here saw it. A million people saw it.'

'Yes,' he said. 'Yes, yes.' You can't get away from the past, he thought, you can't get away from the kind of person you are – or were, if the tense held any significance.

'Then they cut us off. Your poke at Mekles

just grazed him, worse luck. One of his thugs caught you on the face. You fell over, brought down the camera, and it hit your head. Exit one personal investigator, brought home by research assistant to his ever-loving mistress, who bandaged the head. Exit also TV technicians, in confusion.'

'And Mekles?'

'Also exit Mekles, but not as quickly as he expected. He was leaving England tomorrow, changed his mind and wanted to leave tonight, but police questioning kept him till three this morning.'

'Police questioning?' His head was aching badly.

'He can't talk,' Anna said. 'He doesn't feel like talking. I won't have him worried.'

The French clock on the mantelpiece said five minutes past six. He had slept, then, most of the night.

'He needn't talk, but he'd better listen.' There was an edge to Charlie's voice. 'I've had the telephone cut off, but you're an object of interest at the moment. To newspapermen. And the police. We stalled them last night, but they'll be round this morning.'

He felt utterly confused. 'Because of–?'

'We started transmitting at nine-thirty last night, right? You asked Mekles questions about this and that, and then asked him about a man named Bond. You implied that Mekles had come over here to do business with him, right? Where did you get the dope on that?'

'From your research notes.' The question held little reality for him. The past had him, gripped him like a pair of pincers.

'But I told you it was background stuff. I told you not to use it,' Charlie cried in exasperation. He took out a toothpick, put it in his mouth, bit through it, threw it away and took another.

Imprisoned in his dream of the past he said idly, 'Does it matter?'

'This much.' Charlie rolled the toothpick quickly to the corner of his mouth. 'You quizzed Mekles about Bond in the programme. Rather more than three hours earlier – just after six o'clock to be precise – Bond jumped out of the window of his flat. He lived in a block near Marble Arch. You didn't know that?'

'Of course not.'

'He was dead when he hit the ground. It was in the late evening papers, a paragraph.'

Anna watched him anxiously. His mental processes were sluggish, he could only think about the past. 'And so?'

'So it looked as though you knew about Bond's death and were accusing Mekles of being implicated in it. Naturally he was riled. But the point is this, Bill. I hoped you might have some good reason for mentioning Bond, beside the guff in my notes. But you hadn't? Nothing at all?' Charlie threw up his hands. 'Then we're up the creek.'

The doorbell rang.

Chapter Five

No doubt they were up the creek, as Charlie had said, but they were hardly up equal distances. It was nice of Charlie to make the disaster inclusive, but really for him it was no more than a matter of losing one pretty well-paid research job out of a dozen. For Hunter it was another thing, although not one which he could yet take seriously. To the policeman who talked to him he patiently but rather absently repeated that he had no basis for making the remark about Bond other than the research notes of his assistant, Mr Cash.

This policeman was a slick young man, who had the brisk, confiding air of an insurance or even a vacuum cleaner salesman. When he spoke it was with a slightly apologetic air, as though he were trying to sell you something, and knew that it was an article of inferior quality, because unfortunately he did not work for the very best firm. He had this air now as he read the note on Bond made by Charlie Cash.

'These notes were not much more than

gossip, as Mr Cash has admitted. You agree about that?'

'Yes. The interview was not going well. I was trying to get some reaction from Mekles.'

The police inspector, whose name was Crambo, shook his head in apparent puzzlement. 'They call me Dumb Crambo at the Yard, and I'm not surprised. I would never have suspected that you'd ask a question in that way, just on a basis of gossip.'

'Well, I did,' Hunter said wearily.

'If it had been someone like me, now, someone stupid, I should have been afraid of slander. But I suppose you put the questions very cunningly, eh?'

'I don't know that I worried about that. The question itself was harmless, just a suggestion that Mekles was doing business with Bond. I was surprised by the way he reacted.'

'Harmless,' Crambo said meditatively. 'That's assuming you didn't know that this chap Bond had dived out of his window earlier that evening.'

'I didn't know it. I hadn't seen a paper.'

'But Mr Mekles had seen a paper, he told me so himself, and he didn't like it at all. Natural that he shouldn't like it, don't you agree.'

'I suppose it was.'

'All quite natural, you might say. Your

innocent question and his feeling that you were needling him, you might say.' He said suddenly, 'When did you first meet Bond?'

'I didn't know him from Adam.'

'I expect you'd have known him from Eve,' Crambo said, and looked shamefaced. 'You'll have to pardon me. My sense of humour gets the better of me at times. Then Mr Mekles makes this nasty remark about *you.*'

'Yes. I–'

Crambo gave a twist to the trousers of his neat grey pin-stripe suit. 'We know all about that. There's no need to explain. A bit of bad luck for you, if I may say so. I've always admired your programme, you know.' Hunter mumbled something. 'Indeed, I have. I always say to the little woman, "Turn it on now, Doreen, mustn't miss the Personal Investigator." I like a programme with a punch. Next to Dragnet, you're my favourite. The way that man Friday goes on – oh, there I am again, *man Friday*, do you see? I apologise.'

'Did Bond commit suicide?' Hunter asked, in an attempt to put a stop to this clowning.

'No doubt about it. A witness opposite saw him clamber out on to the sill and jump.'

'Why did he do it?'

'That's what we'd like to know.' Crambo's glance was suddenly remarkably keen. 'I should value your ideas about that, you know.'

But Hunter had no ideas. When Crambo left after an hour and a quarter, his professional salesman's cheerfulness seemed to mask slight disappointment.

After Crambo came the reporters, but he disappointed them too by his blank serenity and artificial calm, as well as by his refusal to say anything about past or future. He said only one thing that interested them.

'Mr Hunter,' said the owl-faced crime reporter of the *Banner*, 'a certain accusation was made against you last night by Mr Mekles.'

'You mean he said that my name was O'Brien, and I had been in prison?' Their pens pointed eagerly at the pads in their hands. Their faces had an identical expression of Pavlovian doggy pleasure at the rung bell when he said almost indifferently, 'What he said was true.'

He refused all further details, he refused an offer of money for his life story, he refused to say whether he would resign his job. They left, dissatisfied after all. There had been the bell ringing, the salivation, but in the end no food. Within a few hours there would be food enough, Hunter thought. They hadn't long to wait.

After the reporters, with the telephone reconnected, came Jerry Wilton, sepulchral, sad, inviting him to attend a committee meeting to discuss his position that very afternoon.

Calmly he said, 'You don't really want me coming along, Jerry. I don't want to be an embarrassment. I'll sit down and write my resignation now.'

He could hear relief as well as sympathy in Jerry's voice, as he said that Bill understood the whole thing, taking it like a sportsman, wanted to be absolutely fair, must consider public, duty we all owe, hoped remain good friends. Jerry did not mention O'Brien or prison, and Hunter guessed that he knew all about it, and knew what O'Brien had gone to prison for. But Jerry did proceed to dot the i's and cross the t's when he mentioned the disgrace clause in the contract, and added that strictly speaking it could be invoked, but nobody wanted to do a thing like that, remain good friends, resign and be paid six months' salary.

There was a question mark in Jerry's voice. Hunter guessed that he might have got more by bargaining, but he did not want to bargain. 'That's very generous,' he said, and meant it.

Jerry was pleased. Jerry's voice had changed a great deal from its artificial opening grace notes, changed almost to his ordinary, equally artificial, back-slapping geniality, as he said that the whole thing was a great pity, a damned shame, he blamed himself a good deal, they must have a drink sometime. Hunter agreed that they must have a drink sometime, and added mentally, sometime never.

Chapter Six

And after Jerry there was Anna, facing him now with the look of a bitch that knows something unpleasant is going to happen, afraid that she is going to be put to sleep. Anna, a blonde, not dumb but sluttish, a girl who powdered in the good eighteenth century way instead of bathing, a girl who left her hairpins in the bed. Anna, who wore expensive but vulgar clothes, who had taken lessons at the Cordon Bleu Cookery School but still left slugs in the salad. Anna, who at twenty-eight showed no wrinkles round her big blue eyes, but was losing her figure through indulgence in chocolates. But Anna, also, willing companion of bed and never bored, never bad-tempered, faithful although ineffective cosseter in time of trouble. What did one do about Anna, who wanted marriage but bravely pretended that she liked living in sin, Anna who now sat looking at him fearfully while one hand, with a pretence at disembodiment, conveyed a liqueur chocolate to her mouth.

'Anna.' She started, as though a statue had spoken. One or two drops from the chocolate went on to her frock. 'Three and a half years, Anna. It's a long time.'

Tears welled easily into her eyes, as they are said, inaccurately, to come into the eyes of babies. 'You're going to leave me.'

He stood up to look at himself in the glass and saw a burly figure, a bruiser's face with its blunt features and a squashed nose. The neck was thick, ropy, the body big and clumsy. The ridiculous bandage topped it. When he pulled off the bandage thick reddish hair sprang up eagerly. On his forehead there was a bump, no blood.

'But why? Don't you like me any more?' Now the tears rolled. They did not make her look unsightly. Glycerine tears could not have made less impact on the smooth glow of her cheeks.

'Three and a half years since that night at Biff Ellerby's party.' Biff Ellerby was a minor band leader and Hunter, who was on the news desk of an evening paper, had been invited to the party at second hand, by the paper's radio critic. There he met Anna, wearing a blue frock the simplicity of which she had not quite been able to spoil by adding to it a number of chains and trinkets. There had been, there still was, a softness and pliability about her. He had immediately christened her, mentally, the Dunlopillo girl. She was a commercial artist, she told him, a freelance doing work for an agency, but that was only temporary, she did serious paintings as well and they were so much more interesting, really, didn't he agree?

Hunter was enchanted. He went home with her that night, and appreciated the untidiness of her flat off Marylebone Road, the knickers left in the lavatory, the six unfinished canvases sweating in the bathroom. He moved there next day, bringing his few belongings in a battered blue suitcase. Within a week she had given up the freelance work to concentrate, as she said, on real painting, but somehow the real paintings – portraits of him and of their friends, still lifes, abstractions – turned into rather bad commercial art, just as her most wholehearted attempts to produce purely commercial work were touched, and in a way spoiled, by her dim knowledge of something better. But she had made enough money out of her work as a freelance to live independently of horrified parents in Ealing, and no doubt – he told himself – she would always earn enough to keep herself in comfortable disorder.

'Why do you want to go? I don't see.'

How could he explain? 'After what happened last night there's no room for me in

TV, you understand that.'

'But you could go back to a newspaper.'

'Or in newspapers.' He hesitated, but the impulse to self-revelation was too strong, the current of the past carried him along with it. He said it baldly. 'I spent ten years in jail. For murder.'

'For murder.' Her hand groped instinctively for another chocolate, then moved rejectingly away.

'I was in the IRA when I was a boy. In the thirties. We were in what they called a fund-raising group. We came over to England, three others and I, and we robbed a big store in Manchester. The night watchman found us, there was a fight, and I shot him. I never meant to kill him,' he said protestingly. 'You believe that, don't you?'

She said nothing, but took a chocolate, put it into her mouth.

'I got a life sentence. Pardoned after ten years. That's all.' That was the story, and with what miraculous compression he had told it, leaving out so much, the days on bread and water, the nights when he had prayed, truly prayed, for a bomb to hit the prison and kill every living thing in it, the other times when he had gone over and over the raid on the store and seen how ludicrously careless it had been, the absolutely inadequate precautions taken against possible discovery by the watchman – and then had replanned it in his mind so that the whole thing went like a charm, the watchman was taken out and filled with drink or drugs, the exit and getaway were elaborately planned so that within twelve hours they were back in Eire...

'What was that?' he asked. Anna had said something.

'You must have believed in it. To take a risk like that.'

'Believed in what?'

'Why, I don't know. A united Ireland.'

He laughed, and Anna, who knew that social questions were important, looked offended. How was it possible to explain that it was not really a matter of belief at all, that one did certain things regardless of their effects, things that affected, totally and catastrophically, one's whole life? What had the Movement, as they called it, meant to him? An organised unruliness that offered release from the strict dreariness of his Dublin home, his drunken prayer-saying father and invalid mother. It might have been the Boy Scouts, jamborees and clasp knives, it might have been emigration and the British army. But by chance, or rather by chances, a fine network of interlacing chances, this boy known at school, that one met casually in a pub, it had been the Movement, secret meetings, the necessity for terrorism explained and accepted, the virtue of robbery for the

Movement taken for granted. And then the smoke going up from the revolver that he had fired no more than a dozen times in all, and suddenly the decisions were made and the illusion of choice, by which so many of us live, was gone.

'It wasn't like that,' he said. 'It wasn't like that at all.'

'You didn't believe?'

'I don't know. But that didn't matter.'

'Didn't matter?' she echoed wonderingly. 'But of course it mattered. It was the only important thing.'

'There are certain things you do,' he said slowly. 'And there's no going back on them. Even when you do them by accident–'

'You didn't mean to shoot?'

He waved a hand in an attempt to brush away her literalness. 'I meant to shoot, yes.'

'Then it was murder.'

'It was murder,' he said earnestly, 'but I might just as well have missed, do you understand that? The raid might have succeeded, we could have got back safely.'

'There could have been other raids. One day you'd have been caught.'

Again her words seemed to him almost irrelevant. 'You do something, you do it almost by accident, and you never get away from it all the rest of your life.'

'It wasn't an accident,' she said obstinately. 'You said you meant to shoot. But it doesn't matter to me.'

She was sitting now on the sofa beside him, and he looked with sudden tenderness at the soft, grimy hand, with its line of dirt under the nail. 'You never get away from it, but you have to try. That's what I've always thought. That's why I didn't tell you about it.'

'It would have been bad luck, is that what you mean?'

'Something like that. But you don't understand, nobody can.' The problems of having no past history, no references, no union card, were impossible to explain. But still, he tried. 'O'Brien's my real name, but not the one I was using on the raid. I was arrested and tried under the name of Hartley. That's why the papers haven't made the link-up yet. But they will soon, probably today. It'll be a front page story for a couple of days, the convicted murderer who ran a personal investigation programme on the telly. And after it, I'm finished, you see that.' He found himself anxious, after all, to convince her of it, to show her the futility of struggle.

'But you did it once.' She would not give up easily.

'I was lucky. Met Charlie and worked out the personal investigation idea with him, he knew Jerry and got it a trial run. You know all that.'

'You might be lucky again.' He did not

trouble to reply. Almost timidly she asked, 'What are you going to do?'

'I shall go underground.' He was annoyed when she giggled. 'Change my name. Go abroad, perhaps.'

'Go to Africa.'

'Perhaps.'

'And shoot big game.' Now, on the sofa beside him, she rocked with laughter. These sudden changes of mood, which had once charmed him, now seemed merely distractions. But she dropped back quickly into seriousness, tears glistened becomingly on the plump cheeks. 'Why can't you take me with you, wherever you're going? I won't be any trouble. I love you, Bill.'

There it was, the direct and naked statement. He felt himself moved by it, yet there was an ice block somewhere within that remained unfrozen by the words.

'Ralph would divorce me,' she went on. 'You know that. We could get married.'

He was appalled by the words. To marry was to accept responsibility, and it had always been for him one of Anna's attractions that she had a husband in the background, a plodding, pleading civil servant whom she had left after a year. He wrote to her once or twice a month, offering to divorce her but saying that he loved her still, and asking her to go back to him. Anna sometimes showed him the letters, and one recurrent phrase in them impressed him particularly. 'If you come back we would wipe out the past, and start again with a clean sheet,' the phrase ran, with occasional variations. To wipe out the past – what a fool the man must be even to consider it possible. And now Anna herself, whom he had always thought of as living by and for the minute, was proposing a variation of this *wipe out the past* idea.

'Don't you see,' she said now, 'it's what you want. A fixed point, something to rely on. Don't you see that it's no good running away?'

He shook his head by way of implying what he obviously could not make comprehensible to her, that running away was not the way to talk about it, that for a man like himself life must consist of a series of attempts, however unsuccessful, to break with the past.

'What's the use of talking like that?' he said roughly, and then, more because he knew she expected it from him than because of real concern, added, 'What will you do, Anna?'

'Me?' She seemed surprised. 'Go back to commercial art, I suppose. I might even do some real painting. But you're not worried about me. Why should you be? You don't love me.'

There was evidently to be a scene, and one of the things he had always liked most about

Anna was the fact that she avoided scenes. He felt obscurely, perhaps, that he if anybody had a right to make scenes and that if he, with the shape of his life disastrously decided in youth, made no complaint about it, kept the fact tucked away like the Spartan boy with the fox, others had no right to voice their trivial complaints about the hardness of life and the narrowness of love. Yet he knew that that was what they did, and prepared himself now for Anna's scene, her grand renunciation.

But at the last moment the storm did not break. She got up, walked away from him, smoothed down her skirt over her hips. 'It's whatever you want. It always has been. I'm going out now. I shall be gone for a couple of hours. I want you to be out of here when I get back.'

'Yes.' He was, in a way, cheated by her calmness. 'Don't tell me where you're going. Then I shan't be able to tell the newspapermen who come round asking.'

He said yes again, surprised, almost alarmed, by the placidity on her plump face. She bit a dirty nail.

'There's one thing. Have you thought that you might be giving up too soon?'

'I don't know what you mean.'

'You said you were tried as Hartley. But Mekles called you O'Brien. Where did he get that name from? And for that matter, why did he say what he did about you?'

He shrugged. 'Does it matter?'

'To me it would matter. But to you perhaps it doesn't. You want to think of yourself as one of the lost, and I can't stop you.'

The blow struck too near home for comfort. He wanted to explain that he had no choice in the matter, that what she interpreted as a feeble fatalism was simply acknowledgement of the facts, but she raised her hand in a careless goodbye, and was out of the door and down the stairs before he could marshal the words of explanation. He went to the window and watched her walk in her slovenly heel-scuffing way along the street outside, and then turn in the direction of Baker Street.

He stayed in the room with that disturbing consciousness of something left unsaid. It was Anna's room, not his, with her bad paintings on the walls, her French clock, her collection of foreign dolls staring, dusty and frozen-eyed, from a shelf in one corner, her books, D H Lawrence and Rupert Brooke and *Gone With the Wind* untidily piled on another shelf, her box of darning wools left open with two or three needles from it gleaming on the floor. There was no personal sign of his own occupancy, more than his shaving things and toothbrush in the bathroom, and his clothes in the bedroom wardrobe. She took me into her warm, comfortable life, he thought, and let me become part of it, but now that I am separating myself from her, it will be for her as though I had never been.

He went into the bedroom and began to pack his clothes, taking only as much as would go in the old blue suitcase. One day he would come back for the rest.

Chapter Seven

He went underground by taking a room in the Cosmos, a dubious hotel in Pimlico, just off Wilton Road. Here he registered under the name of William Smith, ate the dreary food, roast beef, mashed and cabbage for lunch, roast lamb, baked and carrots for dinner, sat in the lounge downstairs and watched the tarts come in with their men, or lay on the bed in his mauve-papered room upstairs that looked out over Pimlico chimney pots, and read the papers.

He had been quite right about the newspaper boys quickly making the link between Hartley and O'Brien. Indeed, he had got out only just in time. The evening papers on the day he left the flat were full of it, and the morning papers on the following day elaborated the theme, telling the full story of his original IRA exploit and of night watchman Tibbitt's murder – he had forgotten the name, and now its slight absurdity brought the whole thing back to him, but how extraordinary it was to kill a man and then forget his name. Very naturally, the papers were chiefly concerned with his progress from convicted murderer to television reporter. The evening newspaper for which he had worked ran a special feature of notes by people who had been with him on the news desk, and had apparently made all kinds of interpretations of his character that had not been evident at the time.

He had been engaged after the submission of a series of spoof articles supposed to have been written by a traveller in the Soviet Union. The paper had bought, but never printed, these articles. Somebody had now disinterred one of these from the files, and it was printed, presumably to show the extreme disingenuousness of his character. There was an interview with Jerry Wilton in which he stuck rather bravely to some sort of guns, saying that Bill Hunter had been a very good television interviewer, with fresh ideas and a good technique, and that he had been personally extremely sorry when Bill resigned. In answer to the question, 'Would it have made any difference to you, had you known you were working with a convicted murderer?' Jerry had gallantly replied, 'Not the slightest. I judge people by their behaviour, and Bill was always a good trooper.' Anna was mentioned in a couple of the stories, as his friend. She replied to all questions about where he was, 'He told me he was going away to the country for a complete rest.'

All this was what he had expected, and he was glad to be away from it. There was one other item of interest, a telephone call made by the *Banner* to Mr Nicholas Mekles, at his villa on the Riviera. Mekles, according to the paper, had said:

'I was given the information about Hunter shortly before the interview began. I confess that I was surprised that such a man should be sent to interview me, but I thought it would not be polite to raise an objection at the last minute. During the interview, however, the remarks he made were so insulting that I felt obliged to say something. I had no wish to force his resignation.'

'Why did you refer to him by the name O'Brien when he was tried and convicted in the name of Hartley?' the *Banner* reporter asked.

'I did not wish to cause Hunter unnecessary embarrassment.'

'His suggestions about your business connection with Bond were quite baseless?'

'Quite baseless. As I told the police, I never heard of the man before in my life.'

Lying on his bed and staring up at the

stained, cracked ceiling, he realised that few people would believe that he had asked the question about Bond innocently, merely on the basis of Charlie's research notes. Mekles had naturally considered the remark as a vicious personal attack, and had struck back. But how had he been able to strike back, where did his knowledge come from, how did he know the name of O'Brien? It was common, although not invariable, for members of the IRA to use another name, especially if they were engaged in dangerous work. The police had guessed that Hartley was an assumed name, but had made little attempt to trace his real one. What did it matter, when he was safe inside with a sentence of life imprisonment? He had quarrelled with his parents, and had left home. They had never got into touch with him while he was in prison, and if they had identified their son with the man accused of murder in Britain they had, typically, kept quiet about it.

How, then, had Mekles learned the name O'Brien? When Anna had mentioned this very point he had asked, 'Does it matter?' But now, with knees up on the bed, he found himself mildly curious. Three men had been with him on the job – Craxton, Mulligan and Bert Bailey. They had known his real name, they had all done long stretches. But Mulligan had died in the war, and Craxton had been knocked over by a car and killed five years ago, just after doing a job. That left Bert Bailey – garrulous, stupid Bert Bailey with his whining voice and his interminable stream of hard-luck stories, which he even sprung on the police after his arrest. Could Bert Bailey be working for Mekles? It seemed unlikely and in any case, he repeated to himself as the small spark of curiosity died, what does it matter? Bill O'Brien, alias Bill Hartley, alias Bill Hunter, alias William Smith, he said to himself, you are worrying about something that is no longer any concern of yours. Worn out by the strain of so much, and such depressing, thought, he fell into a light sleep.

Waking, he felt a strangely exhilarating sense of freedom, with a small undercurrent of shame. Freedom: it was something, after all, to have the worst known and said, to have lost temporarily the fear of discovery that had been for years the motive force of his actions. He had committed a crime, he had spent years in prison for it, the offence had been paid for. What was he afraid of, then, why was he hiding like a rat in this stinking hole of a hotel? And the shame was complementary to this feeling, it urged him to start a new life without delay, since that was apparently what he wanted.

Before that, though, he should finish with the old one. Having said goodbye to Anna, he should now say goodbye also to Charlie Cash. He went down to the gloomy lounge, telephoned Charlie and arranged to meet him in a Wilton Road pub. When he got there, Charlie was already at the bar.

'I've been trying to get in touch with you, Bill. Anna said you'd left, she didn't know where you were.' He looked sideways down his long nose. 'She's taking it hard, Bill.'

He shook his head irritably. 'It's better for Anna, as well as for me. We couldn't go on.'

'She doesn't think that.'

'It has to be, Charlie, it's just a thing that has to be. I've got to make a fresh start. Another name, another kind of life. You must see that.'

Charlie made no comment on that. 'I wanted to see you. But tell me what you wanted me for, first.'

'They've given me six months' pay. You've lost a pretty good client, and it wasn't your fault. I ought to pay you something.' Put like that, it sounded offensive, and he was not surprised that Charlie shook his head.

'No need. I've lined up a replacement client already. Besides, if I hadn't given you that stuff about Bond you wouldn't have blown your top. That's what I wanted to talk to you about. Bond, I mean.'

'Bond?' Whatever he had expected, it was not this.

'I know a sergeant at the station, and he

gave me the inside story.' Charlie always knew a sergeant, or an electrician, or an understudy, who could give him the inside story. His life was passed in interpreting hints, putting two and two together, reading something – but was it the truth? – between the lines. 'The police think Bond was being blackmailed.'

He looked at the dark beer in his glass, then wonderingly, up at the barmaid, who returned his stare. It crossed his mind that she might have recognised his picture in the paper. Charlie was talking again.

'This sergeant may have been dropping a story deliberately. You know that inspector on the case, Crambo? He's smarter than he sounds. He may have told the sergeant to drop the story to me, reckoning it would get back to you.' Hunter shook his head vaguely, to show that he did not know or care whether Crambo might have done this. 'But I don't think so.'

Charlie put a toothpick in his mouth, twisted it thoughtfully. 'Bond took dope, that's the way my sergeant boyfriend tells it, probably reefers. He left a note, can't go on and all that. He'd been quite a boy this Bond, in Parliament at twenty-seven, made a splash with his first speech, possible advancement, so on. Then none of it happened and he resigned his seat for reasons of health. Ran this Bellwinder Company, but that was on the skids. Hard up. Now, what does all that add up to?'

He was conscious of pure indifference to Melville Bond, and even to Charlie Cash. 'Does it matter?'

'It matters this much, cock, that the cops have been giving me an uncomfortable time of it this last day or two. Where did my information about Bond come from, that kind of stuff. They seem to take it all pretty seriously.'

'And you told them.'

'Yes, I told them.' Charlie took the toothpick out of his mouth, broke it, put it in an ashtray. 'Trouble is, it's not that simple. There's a geezer I know named Twisty Dodds, kind of a small-time crook you might call him, and I got this story from Twisty, he's got a girl named Maida. Now Maida's cousin is–'

He ceased to listen. Exhilaration about the future filled his mind to the exclusion of anything else. The words, a *clean break*, were repeated over and over. What kind of a break? On the money now in the bank he could live for how many months – six, nine, twelve? – in Spain, Portugal, Austria, Southern Italy. He would settle there, merge imperceptibly into the life of the country. O'Brien, Hartley, Hunter, Smith, they would all become one anonymous figure living peacefully in the country of his choice...

A name brought him back. 'What's that?' he asked. 'What did you say?'

Charlie looked surprised. 'I just told you. This sister of Maida's cousin, this Queenie, is going about with a man named Paddy Brannigan.'

Paddy Brannigan. The name brought with it a face, square and vicious, young, with expressionless grey eyes. Captain Brannigan of the Irish Republican Army, Captain Brannigan who had told them just what to do and how to do it. Captain Brannigan, not long out of his teens himself, who had given a boy a gun and told him to use it.

'Brannigan. You said Brannigan?'

Charlie looked at him sideways, slyly. 'That's right. You know him?'

'Yes.'

'Well, Brannigan told this girl he was working for Mekles, see. I told the police that.'

'What did they think of it?'

Charlie's mouth turned down in mock self-deprecation. 'Not much.'

'Have the police been in touch with him?'

'How would I know? The sergeant didn't tell me. There's another thing, Bill.'

'Yes?'

'I don't want you to think I'm sticking my nose in. Though you may say it's long enough.' Charlie grinned.

'I didn't say it.' He didn't grin back.

'You're not treating that girl right, Bill, running out on her the way you have. A lovely girl like that. It's none of my business, really.'

'You're right there.'

'But I've got to say it. You're not treating her right, a girl like that. I call it a damned shame.'

He said nothing. Charlie drained his glass and ordered another. 'PMYOB, is it? All right, you don't have to say it out loud. But I wanted to talk to you about Bond.'

'What about him?'

'There doesn't seem any doubt it was suicide, but still there was something rotten in the state of Denmark. Suppose you and I took a looksee to try and find out something.'

'Can it do any good? I don't see the point.'

'Hard to tell whether there's any point,' Charlie said carefully. 'May be a waste of time. Half the things we do are a waste of time if you ask me. Won't get you your job back, that's for sure. But if we turned up something that put you in the clear with the police, it wouldn't do any harm. Wouldn't do me any harm either, to tell you the truth.'

Suddenly he felt warmly affectionate towards Charlie, aware of the utterly unassuming nature of his friendship. 'Let's look around,' he said. 'And thanks.'

'Hoped you'd say that. I fixed an appointment for us to see the caretaker of Bond's block of flats. In half an hour. Just got time for another pint.'

Chapter Eight

Bond had lived in a large block of anonymous flats, a greyish slab at the back of Marble Arch. The caretaker, to Hunter's surprise, was a woman, a dark square-faced motherly woman in her forties named Mrs Williams, who watched with apparent fascination the toothpick that shuttled from side to side of Charlie's mouth. But although fascinated she was cautious. 'I've told the police everything, of course. And newspapermen too. What would you gentlemen be wanting information for, now?'

Charlie rolled the toothpick frantically. His explanation was voluble but confused. Hunter caught words and phrases. '...journalists ... my editor said ... something more behind it, Cash, than simple ... heart of the mystery ... get right down there and find out...' He took out his wallet, but the woman's eyes showed no gleam at sight of the notes with which it was stuffed.

She seemed merely puzzled. 'I've got my work to do, you know, but I don't mind answering questions if they don't take too much time. But there's no mystery that I know of. Mr Bond jumped out of the window, poor man, and that's all there is to it.'

'Ah, but why did he jump?' Charlie put his head on one side as he asked the question, to which he immediately added another. 'Did you know that he took drugs?'

'I did not. But how would I have done? I used to clean up there for an hour every day, but I never saw anything suspicious. For the matter of that, I probably wouldn't have recognised it anyway.'

'You cleaned up the flat,' Charlie said in an astonished voice, rather as if she had told him she performed a daily miracle. In what was almost a whisper he said, 'Would it be possible for us – my friend here and I – to have a look over it?'

She looked doubtful, and he again produced the wallet. This time she spoke decisively. 'You can put that thing away, and stop flashing your money at me. I'm an honest widow, Mr Cash, quite satisfied with what I get from my job here. If I show you the flat it's because I like your looks, and not for money.'

'You mean you're going to let us see it? Bless you, ma'am.' Charlie split his long body in a bow, so that his head almost touched the floor.

'You don't go prying about in there alone, mind. I'll be in there with you. I know what you're like, you journalists. Not a scrap of honesty among the lot of you. Rob your own mothers to get a story.' She spoke almost affectionately.

'Did he have many visitors?' Hunter asked as they went up in the lift.

'How should I know? They come in, get into the lift, press the button. No reason for me to see them, or them to see me.'

They got out, walked along the corridor, stopped in front of a door.

'What sort of a man was he?'

'What sort of a man?' She had taken out a key and put it in the lock. Now she turned it. 'Work it out for yourself.'

The flat consisted of a living room, bedroom, bathroom and kitchenette. It had, like so many such flats, an utter lack of individuality. The furniture was of good quality, but might have come from any big department store. The books in two small cases were book club editions. A desk stood in one corner of the room. Charlie moved over towards it, delicately touched the top, looked out of the corner of one eye at Mrs Williams, and coughed.

'It's locked,' she said.

'That needn't bother us.' He jingled keys in his pocket, grinned.

'You see,' she appealed delightedly to

Hunter. 'Just as I said, not a scrap of honesty. Think nothing of opening a dead man's desk, going through his belongings. But it's no good. Even if I was to let you do it, you'd find nothing. The police have been through it already.'

'Did they find anything interesting?'

'Not that I know of. Then Mrs Riddell – that's Mr Bond's sister, his nearest relative – came in, too. She took away some papers. There'd be nothing interesting left now.'

'I'd like to make sure of that.' Charlie put his head on one side, rolled the toothpick. 'Haven't you got something important to do in another flat now? Just for ten minutes.'

'No,' she said emphatically.

Hunter crossed to the window. 'He jumped from this one?'

'Yes.'

The sill was fairly low, the window a modern iron-framed one that opened outwards. It would be easy enough to step on to the outer sill and jump. There were no marks on the sill outside. Inside, two long scratches had torn the wallpaper below the sill. Hunter bent to look at them, and then asked Mrs Williams if they were new.

'They are. The police asked me the same thing.'

'Come and look at these, Charlie. See what you think of them.' Charlie Cash came over, looked, said nothing. 'Hard to see why anybody getting on the sill to jump out of the window should make marks like that.'

Charlie nodded. He hardly seemed to be listening.

'But if Bond was being forced out, pushed out backwards, then his heels might catch on the wallpaper as he struggled. Nobody heard any sound of a struggle?' he asked the housekeeper. 'The people in other flats, I mean.'

'No. You might not think it, but these flats are very well insulated for sound. You don't hear the radio from one flat in another.' She sniffed. 'Not that in this case there was anything to hear, if you ask me. He jumped. That was the verdict at the inquest, wasn't it.'

'Yes. You're forgetting something, Bill.' Charlie was staring across the street, at a tall, narrow building opposite.

'What's that?'

'There was a witness. In that block over there. Somebody who saw Bond jump.'

They moved away from the window. Mrs. Williams had said they could work out for themselves what sort of a man Bond was. What had she meant?

The bedroom seemed at first sight to give no more hint of a personality than the living room. The suits hanging in the wardrobe were well made, conspicuously elegant. Several pairs of shoes stood at the bottom of the wardrobe, in different colours of suede. A chest of drawers contained silk underclothing, and several silk shirts.

Charlie whistled. 'Beauty gallery. Come and look.'

Over the divan bed were photographs of half a dozen boys and young men, all rather consciously posed against backgrounds of sea or country landscape. Three of them wore open neck shirts, two wore bathing shorts, one was naked. All of the photographs were signed in scrawling, unformed hands. Hunter read, 'For Mel, with love from Jack.' 'For my friend Mel, from Jimmy boy.'

On a small mantelpiece were some photographs of Bond. One showed him outside the Houses of Parliament – he had been elected in 1945, Hunter remembered – looking spruce, dapper, younger than his twenty-seven years. Another photograph showed him bouncing a ball on the beach, with one of the boys in the photographs over the bed. A third, obviously much more recent, was of a gaunt, baggy-eyed figure, hardly recognisable as the man standing outside the House of Commons.

Was this what Mrs Williams had meant? Evidently it was. She stood now with her hands clasped together, eyes looking modestly at the floor.

When they were outside Hunter said, 'So

now we know that he was a homosexual, as well as taking drugs. Nice chap. But how does it help?'

'You're forgetting those heel marks, if that's what they were. The ones you thought meant there'd been a struggle.'

'The police won't have missed them. They're not fools. And what can we do about them anyway?'

'We can see what Miss Tanya Broderick thinks.'

'Who's Miss Tanya Broderick?'

They had crossed the road. Charlie spat out his toothpick and pushed open the door to the entrance hall of the narrow building. 'She calls herself a fashion model. And she's the witness who saw Bond jump out of the window.'

Chapter Nine

The flat was on the third floor. Charlie began to talk as soon as the blonde girl opened the door. 'My name's Rogers, Miss Broderick, I'm with the *Daily Banner* on features. This is my colleague, Jack Hunt. We wondered if you'd be interested in giving us a story.'

'A story about me? For your paper?' She had the small, precise voice of a little girl.

'Come in.'

For a moment Hunter had the disconcerting impression that he was in Bond's flat again. The same bookcases with the same book club editions, the same, or very similar furniture. But there were some differences, a telephone covered by the dress of a large French doll, several other dolls in various dresses around the room, a number of tiny glass animals on a table. Miss Broderick herself was tiny, with blonde hair cut in a fringe, a smooth-skinned babyish face, and hard blue eyes.

'I know newspapermen like beer,' she said in that curious, quite artificial little voice. 'But beer always makes me want to keep on spending pennies. There's gin or whisky. But why ever should your newspaper want to do a feature story about me?'

Charlie took out a notebook. 'Tell me now, I haven't got it wrong, you are the Miss Broderick who gave evidence in the case of Melville Bond, aren't you?'

She was pouring whisky, and had her back turned to them. 'Yes.'

'We're doing a series called "The Vital Witness,"' Charlie said. 'People who actually saw what happened during a vital moment in a crime –,

'But there wasn't any crime.'

'Of course not, I didn't mean that. It's just that some of the other cases are of witnesses who actually saw crimes being committed, and without them the evidence would have been incomplete. Or there'd have been no case.'

She brought over the whisky to them. Her fingernails, Hunter saw as she put down the glass by his side, were enamelled bright green to match her dress. 'I see what you mean. But then there wasn't any case, was there? He just jumped out of the window, that's all. I mean, it isn't interesting.'

'There's only your word for it,' Charlie Cash said. He's pushing it too hard, Hunter thought, that was a silly thing to say. But there was no change in her baby face. 'The whole thing might be a bit of a mystery if you hadn't just happened to be at your window at the time.'

Hunter walked across to her window and looked out. It was certainly possible to see what was going on opposite. A man climbing out would have been visible, not only from these flats but from the street. Voicing his thought he said, 'Funny that nobody in the street saw him.'

'People don't look up when they're in the street. Not unless it starts raining, and then they look up to make sure it really is rain and not birds doing their business. People call that luck, but I never could see it.' Her laugh tinkled, tinny as an aluminium bell.

'But you were looking up.'

'Why, it's not just eye level here, but I didn't have to look up much. I was at the window, you see, because it had come over a bit dark and I wondered if it was going to rain.' Her laugh tinkled again. 'Let's not talk about all that, shall we, till we've talked about money. What would the *Banner* pay me for this story?'

'You'd get a lot of publicity,' Charlie said. 'Good for a model. Who do you model for, by the way?'

'I'm a freelance. I don't know whether this is the sort of publicity that does a girl any good. Come on now, Mr Rogers, how much?'

Charlie took out a toothpick, put it in his mouth. 'Fifty is what they told me, but they might spring a hundred.'

'For an exclusive story like that.' Hunter thought he heard mockery in her voice. 'Why, Mr Rogers, I'm disappointed.'

'Look,' Charlie said. 'If the story's good enough, the money will be all right. We're just here to make preliminary inquiries.'

'But I told the police the story. I was getting ready to go out with my boyfriend and I crossed over to the window to see if it was raining and there was this man opposite who'd just pushed his window open and was getting out on to the ledge. I just stood there with my mouth open all ready to scream, but I was simply petrified and the scream just wouldn't come. And then he jumped. And I screamed.'

A faint, subdued buzzing could be heard. She crossed with small steps to the French doll, and lifted it to disclose a telephone of the same green as her nails. She lifted the receiver in a tiny fist.

'Hallo. Why, hallo, darling. No, I can't quite manage that, I'm all in a dither here with two men just now. Oh, I didn't mean that at all. Why, they're reporters.' She went on talking. A pencil in her fingers made patterns on the engagement pad in front of her. From a yard away Hunter read upside down a name written on the pad. The letters said y-d-d-a-P. She looked up, turned one page of the pad and began another pattern.

'What's that you say? Why, what a suspicious mind you've got, honeypie. In half an hour then.' She put down the receiver, replaced the doll and said, 'That was my boyfriend then, I expect you guessed. He says I should ring the *Banner* to see if you really come from it. He says that's just a story you've been telling me, you're probably just trying to make me say something that will get me into trouble. I do hope that isn't right.'

'We're not from the police, if that's what he means,' Charlie said. 'Nothing to do with them.'

'You see. I told him he had a suspicious

mind. But I don't think I'd better say any more, do you? I don't want to get into any trouble. After all, a girl's got her living to earn.'

'Just one question, Miss Broderick,' Hunter said. 'If you don't mind answering it. How long have you been here?'

'Why should I mind?' She looked down at her green nails. 'I've been here nearly three weeks.'

When they were outside Charlie said, 'Three weeks. She'd been there three weeks. It could have been a plant.'

'She had the name Paddy written down on her pad. When she saw me looking at it she turned the sheet.'

Charlie bit on his toothpick and it broke. He threw it away. 'These things aren't what they were. They don't make 'em tough now. This is how it could have been worked. Mekles or his agent, this Paddy of yours, puts this girl in the flat specially to give false evidence. Bond gets pushed out of the window, and she says he jumped. Simple as that. Tell you what, why don't I tail her when she goes out, find out who her boyfriend is?' Hunter shook his head.

'Why not?'

'She never believed a word you said from the start.'

'You don't think so?' Charlie looked indignant. 'She's not a fool, not by any means.

She was stringing us along for the fun of it, or to find out who we were. She's smart enough to know you're tailing her and to give you the slip. And if you did find out she was mixed up with Mekles, what are you going to do then? Don't you suppose the police know it already?'

Charlie looked at him, his thin head on one side. 'Bill, if I ever used long words, I should call you a defeatist.'

How was it possible to make Charlie understand? 'It's no use, Charlie, don't you see that? It's past history. Or at least, it is for me. It just doesn't mean anything any more.'

Chapter Ten

That was Thursday. On Monday of the following week he met Anthea Moorhouse for the first time.

It was boredom that took him to the Victoria Dance Rooms. Until he received the promised cheque it was impossible for him to go abroad, and a strange inertia overcame him. He was reluctant to get in touch with his former employers. To do so, it seemed to him, would be somehow a betrayal of his plans for the future. And now he began to have doubts about that future itself and to ask whether he would really know any kind of happiness alone in a foreign country. The weather remained extremely fine. It was intolerably hot in his bedroom, yet he lacked the energy to move from the Cosmos. Ought he to get in touch with Crambo, say what he knew about Paddy Brannigan? Somehow he lacked the energy for that too.

On Saturday he spent the day at Roehampton Swimming Pool, on Sunday he went to Brighton. The newspapers had dropped the story, and he remained unrecognised. But life after Saturday and Sunday stretched before him, an endless ribbon on which something had to be written. It was to inscribe something on the ribbon, however trivial, that he went to the Victoria Dance Rooms.

They were down a side street, five minutes' walk from the Cosmos. Two teddy boys lounged by the entrance. They wore long draped jackets and narrow trousers beneath which bright pink socks showed. As Hunter turned the corner of the street a long low car pulled up and two couples got out, young men and women in evening clothes. The teddy boys whistled appreciatively and said something as the couples went in. One of the young men, short, dark and sullen, turned back as if to speak to them, but the girl with him pulled him on.

Hunter gave the boys a savage scowl as he passed.

Inside the hall was hot, crowded, dingy. At one end of it Billy Bell and his Boys, six of them, were playing. There was an MC wearing a dinner jacket. Almost all of the couples on the floor were young, and danced locked together. A few unattached girls – would they be hostesses? – sat in the corner chewing gum. The lighting was dim.

He sat out one dance, then moved towards the hostesses. He had hoped to pick up a friendly girl here, a girl with whom he could sit afterwards and talk for half an hour, but that seemed unlikely. One dance and I'll go, he told himself. Then he noticed in the gloom a girl sitting by herself. He stopped and said, 'Will you dance?'

She was, he saw now, one of the girls who had got out of the car.

'That would be fun.' Her voice was light and musical. 'Roger's gone off and left me alone in this den of vice.'

'Is it a den of vice?'

'Didn't you know? That's why we came along, thought it might be fun.' When they were on the floor she nodded at a couple who swayed past them in a clinch. 'You don't expect me to dance like that?'

'I don't expect anything.'

For a moment her body pressed against him, breasts, stomach, thighs. Then she withdrew. 'Why did you do that?' he asked.

'I wanted to see what it was like.'

'And what was it like?'

'Pretty much as I expected.' She threw back her head as she laughed, so that he saw white teeth, pink throat, strong white neck. Her hair was black and long, her mouth well shaped, her head came above his shoulder. 'What are you thinking?'

'I was thinking that Roger's foolish to leave you out of his sight.'

She laughed, and called across to what Hunter recognised as the other couple, 'I've been picked up. Where's Roger? He'll be mad when he comes back.'

The other girl was an insipid blonde. 'He went thataway.'

When they had moved apart from the others he said, 'I'm not sure I like being talked about as if I weren't there.'

'Don't be so sensitive. Oh, my God, Roger's at it again. He really is a bore.'

Turning, he saw that the dark, sullen young man was standing in the entrance to the room and that the two teddy boys were with him. They were talking, it seemed, quietly and earnestly in low voices. 'I don't see anything wrong.'

'You will. Roger's a ju-jitsu expert. He loves trouble.'

As she spoke, one of the teddy boys reached into his hip pocket and came out with a knife. His hand with the knife in it moved upwards. In the same moment Roger took hold of him, quite lightly, by the arm. Then the teddy boy was on the floor, the knife rattled against the wall. Somebody screamed.

'Showing off,' the girl said. She sounded pleased.

The screams did not stop. They got louder, and suddenly he saw the reason. There were two, half a dozen, a dozen policemen in the doorway, now in the room, shouting something unintelligible. At the other end of the room Billy Bell and his Boys were also shouting. Hunter saw the drummer from the band open a door at the side of the stage.

'Come on,' he said to the girl, and she followed him. He pushed open the door and they found themselves in a little changing room. The drummer, a skinny blond boy with big spectacles, looked up. 'Yes,' he said. 'What do you want?'

There was a small window, almost a skylight, high up in the wall. Hunter stood on a table under it, reached up and pushed. The window stuck at first, then opened so suddenly that he almost put his hand through it. Hunter levered himself up, squeezed through with difficulty, and saw that the drop was no more than a few feet. There was no policeman in sight. He looked back and down, and spoke to the girl. 'After me. Not much of a drop. I'll catch you.'

'Come on, mate,' the drummer called. 'Haven't got all day.'

He had a glimpse of the girl's face below him, strained and earnest. Then he dropped, suffering nothing worse than a slight jarring sensation as he landed. He saw the girl above him, and held out his arms. He half caught her, but she landed awkwardly, and there was a splintering noise. She took his hand and they ran.

As they turned the corner into a narrow road he heard a police whistle. He saw that she was hobbling.

'What's the matter?'

'I've snapped the heel off my shoe. I can't run properly.'

'Take them off. I live near here.'

She slipped off the shoes, and carried them in her hand. They turned left and right, with the police whistles still audible behind them, until he saw in front of them the dim blue sign that said Cosmos. He led the way into the gloomy entrance. The man at the desk barely glanced at him as he led the way up the stairs. Probably he was surprised that Hunter had not brought in a girl before this evening.

'You keep a room in this place?' she asked as they went up the stairs.

'I live here.'

'You *live* here.' She did not speak again until he had opened the door of the room and she saw the mauve wallpaper, the stained ceiling, the pocked mirrors and the cracked washbasin. She looked at all these with eager eyes, and then spoke again. 'Why, what fun.'

He said nothing. She sat down on the bed, and said delightedly, 'It squeaks. Why, it's just perfect. Are you a man on the run or something?'

'No. Was the drummer caught?'

'Yes. The police pulled him off the table. He struggled with them, but couldn't get up. It wasn't my fault.'

'I didn't say it was.'

'Do you suppose Roger was caught too? Imagine Roger in court.'

'Just imagine.' He picked up her shoe and looked at it. The heel was snapped off clean. 'I'll call a taxi and put you in it.'

'That would be dull. It's been such an exciting evening so far. Real fun.' She lay back on the bed and it squeaked again. 'Real fun. Don't spoil it.'

He knew that what he was about to do was wrong and dangerous, not morally, but wrong because for him it was somehow nothing to do with any possible future, but part of the chain of the past that he dragged round with him. But he approached the bed, gripped the bare shoulders above the purplish evening dress, bent his face down over hers. Her hands held him back with unexpected strength. Then she laughed.

'Don't look so surprised. You'll spoil my dress.' She stood up, and then in a minute she was out of it.

Afterwards they lay on the bed together. 'There's nobody here to introduce us,' she said. 'We'll have to do it ourselves. My name's Anthea Moorhouse. I expect you know my stepfather.'

Hunter was looking at the ceiling, but not seeing the crack in it. He felt peace and fulfilment, but something more and less than these, a release of tension, an absence of urgency that had been working in him ever since the evening of the fatal telecast. 'Should I know him?'

'Lord Moorhouse. Big shot industrialist. I'm the apple of his eye, even though I've got a rotten core as you might say. He adopted me legally, gave me his name.'

Hunter made a non-committal noise. He felt sleepy. When she spoke again she sounded a little annoyed. 'I keep thinking I know *your* face. What's your name?'

'Bill Smith.'

'Oh, come on.'

'You can look in the register downstairs if you don't believe me.'

'Tell me. Tell me.'

'Bill Smith,' he repeated sleepily. She

pinched him, then leant over him, put her arms round his neck.

'I believe I was right, and you are a criminal. But you can tell me. I can keep a secret. Don't you see, I wouldn't mind, I'd like it even. Don't you see?'

'Bill Hunter.' His defences, for the moment at least, were down. He was not inclined to doubt her, or to ask questions. 'I don't suppose that means anything more to you than your stepfather's name does to me.'

'No. Yes, it does, though.' She sat up beside him, and he put up a hand to touch one of her small breasts. She pushed it away. 'You're the man on TV who asked a lot of questions he shouldn't have done, had a row and resigned. And you killed somebody, that's right?'

'It was a long time ago.' From his own inertia on the bed he lay and watched her face in profile, eager, passionate and determined. Later, perhaps, the nose would become beaky, the lips thin, the jaw jut too formidably, but at this moment she seemed to him exquisitely beautiful. It seemed to him that she was assessing something, making up her mind about something. Then she spoke.

'But that's terrific. To have slept with a man who's killed someone, really killed someone I mean, not just in the war. There can't be many girls who have done that.' She saw the expression on his face. 'Now you hate me. But I want to live, you see. I want to experience everything, do things people haven't done before. Isn't that important?'

'I don't know.'

'To hold life and squeeze the last drop of experience out of it – like that.' She made her small red-nailed fingers into a fist. 'I don't see what else matters.' She swung her legs off the bed and, frowning fiercely, began to put on her clothes.

'Who's Roger?'

'Roger Sennett. I'm sort of engaged to him, or at least that's what my stepfather wants. He's fun too, but I don't know about him. I don't know at all. I don't think I want to get married anyway.'

'You won't tell Roger about the terrific fun you had this evening?'

She shook her head. Irony and sarcasm were wasted on her. 'He wouldn't understand. And anyway, do I want to repeat it? I don't know.'

'Have you ever considered that I might not want to?' The question was a vain one, for he knew that he wanted nothing more.

'But of course if you don't want to see me, why should you?' she said almost impatiently. She had her dress on and was doing her face now in front of the pocked glass. 'I'll just limp out and get a taxi. Don't bother to come down.'

He took refuge in boorishness from his unreasonable disappointment. 'I wasn't bothering.'

'Oh.' In the considering look she gave him he felt her own disappointment, and was immediately slightly ashamed. 'No, don't bother. More romantic like this.' She crossed to the bed, kissed him lightly on the cheek, and then moved with an exaggerated hobble to the door.

Chapter Eleven

The process of falling in love is often painful. Bill Hunter was thirty-eight years old and, in spite of the time lost in prison, had had affairs with several women. None of these affairs, however, seemed to him to have involved the condition of being in love. How was it manifested? During the time after Anthea Moorhouse's visit the recollection of her physical presence was like a rash on his skin. In the rusty bath down the corridor he looked at various parts of his body and thought, here and here she touched me, she held my head tenderly in her hands that want to squeeze sensation out of life, my fingers stroked her ears as I said that they were beautiful.

These thoughts had more of wonder than of sensuality about them, although they were sensual too. He found her face so hauntingly present in his mind that he tried to put it down on paper. He had not tried to draw since winning a prize at school, and now the pencil refused to obey him, so that he created only a caricature of the fine features that were so clear in his mind. The tones of her voice were continually present to him, and he repeated over and over again the phrases she had used, *It was terrific*, *What fun*, and the rest. Submerged beneath this feeling went the knowledge that she was what under any other circumstances he would have called a rich bitch, a girl greedy for pleasure who in some way or other would come to a bad end. He acknowledged formally the existence of a girl like that, but refused to identify her with the girl of his imagination.

He met her on a Monday. On the following morning he read in the paper of 'Raid on Victoria Dance Hall,' and learned that the police had arrested the manager and twenty of the people present. Among those arrested was the Honourable Roger Sennett, second son of Lord Broughleigh, and his friends racing driver Paul Makepeace and society débutante Sabina Brownlee. They had all been released on bail.

He walked round to the public library and

looked up Lord Moorhouse in *Who's Who*. 'Chairman Moorhouse Trust Companies,' he read, 'Vice-Chairman Enterprise Steel Corporation, director Gaines Steel Co., Iron and Steel Foundings, Paine, Lumb Associates, etc., etc. Chairman Patriotic Fellowship Circle. Publications: *The Idea of Empire* (1947), *Hands Across the Colonies* (1953). The personal material was more interesting: 's. of Norman Moorhouse, Leeds; m. 1918 Mary Lavinia, o.d. of Charles Grantham, Mill House, Morningford, Herts.: divorced 1937. m. 1943 Mary Elizabeth Hales, d. 1948.' There was an address in Hampshire, Bassington Old Manor, another in Cavendish Square. There was a telephone number, which he noted down. Then he walked back to the Cosmos and stayed on his bed in a kind of waking dream, evolving fantasies about Lord Moorhouse and evoking again the painful, delightful realities associated with his daughter. That afternoon he took a bus and walked round Cavendish Square, looking at the house in which she lived. Did he hope to see her? or hope that she would come out, accompanied by her stepfather, and introduce him? He could not exactly have said.

That evening he rang her up. She was out. Would he leave a message? Yes, he said carefully, tell her that Mr William Smith telephoned. Perhaps she would call him back when it was convenient. He gave the telephone number of the hotel. As soon as he had put down the receiver he was disgusted with himself. 'Call him back when it was convenient' – what a feeble, vulgar phrase. And to say that he was Mr William Smith – could there be a sillier joke? It was vital in any case, he knew, to keep a sense of proportion, to remember that whatever the affair meant for him, for her it had been no more than an amusing experience. It was possible, likely even, that she would not telephone at all.

She rang next morning. As he ran down the stairs, past the frowsy chambermaid, to the little cubbyhole in the entrance hall where the telephone was kept, he felt his heart beating with an excitement he had not known since, at the age of fifteen, he had first walked out with a girl. Her voice on the telephone had a tone even lighter than he remembered.

'Hallo,' she said. 'Sorry I didn't ring last night. I was at a party, didn't get home till all hours.'

For a moment he found it impossible to speak. Then he was immediately jealous. 'Was it a good party?'

'Terribly boring. Not a bit like Victoria.'

He said breathlessly, 'It was good of you to telephone. I wondered if–'

'Mr William Smith. Such fun. Did you

want to suggest anything, Mr Smith?'

'Could we meet again? Should I call for you?'

'Do you mean here?'

'Yes. I could easily do that.'

'Oh no, I don't think that would be at all a good idea.'

She sounded quite decided. Terrified that she would end the conversation, he said hastily, 'Anywhere you like.'

'Why not the same place?' she said carelessly. 'At three o'clock.'

'If you like. But I could easily meet you somewhere else if you wanted to.'

'Three o'clock. Got to go now. Goodbye.' And she was gone.

Thus began for him an agonisingly painful period of days and weeks. There was a particular image of Anthea in his mind, and it was connected, as he vaguely understood, with the unrealised image of himself, of the life from which he had been cut off by the revolver shot so many years ago. He saw them doing so many things together, visiting Kew Gardens, the Tower of London and Battersea Fun Fair, feeding the ducks from the bridge in St James's Park, listening to the speakers at Marble Arch, going to the sea, spending together days bathed in the sunlight of a primitive innocence pervaded by the presence of physical love. But reality was different. Reality was the squeaking bed at the Cosmos, the bed that was such fun. Reality was this girl who seemed possessed by a wild exhilaration of the senses in which she fought, bit and scratched him. What she wanted was either to come to the Cosmos, or to meet him in dirty little clubs where they met what she called amusing characters, to talk and drink with them for hours, and then return to the Cosmos.

The hotel itself had a fascination for her, and she asked endless questions about its population of ponces, tarts and their clients, with one or two oddities thrown in like boxers down on their luck and faded old young men grubbing a living out of films or the theatre.

'Don't you see, Bill, it's life itself, what goes on here,' she said. Once she angered him by saying that she wished she had had his experience of prison. He told her that she talked like a stupid child, that prison life was utterly destructive of everything decent and sensitive in the personality.

She was unimpressed. 'It doesn't seem to have destroyed the sweetness and light in you, Mr Smith. Rather encouraged it, I should say.'

There were days when the wild irrational gaiety which he thought of as her chief characteristic was totally absent, and was replaced by a morose misery that deeply touched him. On these days her physical appearance changed, the fine features became drawn and unnaturally pointed, and there seemed to be a pleading look in her eyes, as though she were asking him to procure for her something she knew to be unattainable. On days like these his presence seemed to bring her a sort of peace. They would not make love, but she would sit with her legs crossed on the bed and talk about her life at home, the way in which she had been spoilt by her stepfather, and how much she disliked Roger Sennett.

'Daddy wants me to marry Roger. He makes me call him daddy, though he's not my father.'

'Yes, you told me that.'

'It's a good old family he says, he's keen on that like most self-made men. You knew he was a self-made man, that's what they call it, isn't it absurd?'

'Yes.'

'His father was a barber, did you know that?'

'No. Does it matter?'

'It doesn't matter a tuppenny damn to me,' she said unconvincingly. 'But it makes me laugh to think what he'd say if he knew about us.'

'What would he say?' he asked curiously.

She shivered. 'I don't know. He'd – I don't know. And Roger too. Roger would just go wild if he knew about you.'

'He doesn't know anything?'

'If he did he'd kill me. Or you.' She shivered again.

'Why does your stepfather want you to marry him, if you don't want to.'

She bit a red fingernail. 'It's hard to explain. I've had a terrible life. I'll tell you about it one day.'

The statement seemed to him, from the viewpoint of his own life, naïve, absurd even. She said hotly, as though he had contradicted her, 'It's true. You can laugh, but it's true. When I was eleven years old I ran away with a circus, didn't come back for three days. Daddy almost went crazy, offered five thousand pounds reward, had the police out dredging canals and all that.'

'He's fond of you, then.'

'He wanted a son.' She spat out a bit of nail, looked at him out of the corner of her eye. 'Divorced his first wife because they didn't have any children – I mean, that was the real reason. He hoped my mother would have a child by him, but she never did.'

'But he loves you,' Hunter repeated. 'I should have thought it might have worked the other way – he could have hated you.' Again there was that sidewise glance, again he had the sense of something not said, of some meaning beneath the surface of the words.

'Oh, he loves me all right.' She paused. 'In

his own very special kind of way. He wants to own me, wants to run my life. Would you believe it, I don't get an allowance, have to ask him when I want money. I'm twenty-three. Isn't it just crazy, isn't he a crazy man?' She went on,' 'But I fool him. I get money. I do what I want.'

'How do you mean?'

'I'm here with you, aren't I?' The look she gave him was almost sly. 'I hate him, most of the time. I hate him and want to hurt him. But then I love him, too. Or I like him. He's nice. Do you understand that?'

The fact was, as he readily admitted to himself, that he did not understand it or her, that the agonies of spirit she manifestly endured had to him no adequate cause. There were times when she clung to him weeping, and asking him not to let her go. To be regarded by a woman as a pillar of strength was to Hunter a sensation so strange that it gave him a sort of intoxication of pleasure, and pity was joined to the sensual and idealistic love he felt for her. At such times she would talk wildly of committing suicide. Looking with affection at the wretched room in the Cosmos she would say, with no apparent consciousness of absurdity, that it was the nearest thing to home she had ever known.

On one such occasion he began to laugh. She turned on him fiercely. 'Oh, you're a fool. You're just a fool, Bill Hunter. You're so proud of having been in prison. You think you know it all, and the fact is you don't know anything.'

He shrugged, as a substitute for saying that if she liked to believe that she was welcome to do so.

'Do you understand what it is to have the things you love destroyed?' she asked. 'I had a dog once, a spaniel puppy named Troy. I loved that dog more than anything. When I came home from school after my mother died, I was thirteen then, I found that Daddy had had Troy put down. He'd bitten some neighbour's brat who had been teasing him. What do you think of that?'

Hunter shrugged again, to suggest politely that he thought nothing at all of it.

'It seems silly to you, I expect. You're the kind of cold-blooded bastard that it would seem silly to.' And she asked again, 'Do you understand what it is to love someone and hate them at the same time?'

He said slowly, 'I don't think I've ever loved anyone before you. And I don't want to hurt you. If I ever do, it will be by accident.'

During the conversation they had been lying on the bed. Now she rolled over and, burying her head on his chest, began to cry. He tried to raise her head, but she would not look at him. He stroked her black hair.

It was some time before she lifted her head from his chest. 'You don't want to hurt me. You really mean that, don't you?'

'But of course I do,' he said wonderingly.

'You're the first one.' She clung to him, weeping, in an ardour of self-abasement that made her kneel and kiss his hands and feet. 'I love you,' she cried out despairingly, as though she expected contradiction. 'I really love you. What do you want me to do to prove it? Ask me and I'll do it. Anything, anything.'

On the following day she talked to him about her mother and father. 'You know I said you were the first one who didn't want to hurt me. It wasn't true. My father never wanted to hurt me. He did hurt me, but he never meant to. He was Norman Hales. My mother was Mary Hales.'

'I seem to remember your mother's name,' he said uncertainly. 'But I don't know why.'

'Christ, you are an ignorant bastard. Where were you brought up?'

'For ten years I was brought up in prison,' he said mildly. Then he remembered Mary Hales. It was as though a membrane covering and checking the flow of memory broke with the words. He saw again the hall into which they were marched every Thursday for film shows and concert parties. There was always something furtively exciting about those Thursdays. It was not simply that the darkness provided opportunities for exchange of news and the passing of tobacco, but that the two hours during which they were out of their cells always held, for Hunter, an illusion of freedom. In fact nothing ever happened on these Thursdays, there was never any riot or attempt at escape – and if there had been the attempt must have failed, for the hall was packed with warders – yet about those two hours of pretended normality there was undoubtedly the uneasy smell of spurious freedom. It was on one of the Thursdays that Mary Hales, a pretty, fragile blonde, had come down, sung some songs and done a comic sketch as part of a show called – what had it been called now? – the West End Follies. The men had talked about her and the other women, making as usual vivid use of their imaginations. She came back clearly to his mind, a small woman with a pleasant, unremarkable voice and a kittenish sense of comedy, who seemed nervous of her own daring in entering a prison, and yet had something sexually flirtatious in her manner. 'I remember now. She came down once, took part in a show I saw in prison.'

'She was a star, a real star. In musical comedy, I mean. She was beautiful.'

Beautiful? He suppressed the words on his lips, that she had not been nearly so beautiful as her daughter, and said humbly, 'But

I don't remember your father.'

'He was a producer. Norman Hales Productions. *The Girl from St Louis, Song of the Clans, The Girl from Way Back, Esmeralda Went Dancing.'* She spoke the names reverently. 'Mummy starred in some of them. They were all successes. He had a magic touch. Everyone said so.'

Hunter remained silent and she went on talking dreamily, as though he were not there.

'Norman was a most wonderful person. I always called him Norman, he didn't like being called daddy, said it made him feel old. We had a marvellous life, the three of us. They took me about with them everywhere. All over England, France and Italy, once to America. Lots of different hotels, restaurants, always gay, exciting people.'

And you say this room is the nearest thing to home you've ever known, Hunter thought in pity. When he spoke, it was to ask a question. 'You said he hurt you. How did that happen?'

Her face was turned away. 'He never meant to hurt me.'

'You said that too?

'But he was attractive, you know, attractive to women. He had lots of affairs. Sometimes he would go off, we wouldn't see him for a month perhaps. Mother used to cry.' She said rather fiercely, 'I never cried. I knew he'd come back.'

'He loved your mother.'

'He loved *me,*' she said emphatically. 'When he came back he'd just come into the flat – we stayed in lots of flats then, or that's the way I remember it – throw his hat on to a peg and say, "Hallo, Chip, remember me?" That's what he called me, Chip. He'd always come back loaded with presents for both of us, and it would be just as though he'd never gone away.'

'He's dead, isn't he?'

'He was killed in March, 1941. He was walking along during a raid, and a warden told him to take cover. He said –the warden told us about it afterwards – "Thank you for your advice, my dear sir, but I'm already late for an appointment, and I've made a private arrangement with the Germans that they won't bomb the particular district I happen to be visiting. They keep a note of my movements, you know, Lord Haw Haw looks after me in person." He was killed two minutes later by a piece of flying shrapnel. They thought it was from one of our own guns.'

The picture she was building up, of an amorous Peter Pan who didn't like being called daddy, and was facetious and foolhardy during air raids, seemed to Hunter thoroughly dislikeable. It would, he knew, be unwise to say so. 'What did your mother think?' he asked. 'I mean about his affairs, and so on.'

'She accepted them. You just had to accept them. That's the kind of man he was.' They had been drinking in a little club called the Low Down and she sat there now, legs thrust out in front of her, arms hanging loose, head sunk, a picture of clownish dejection so complete as to be comic. 'I was only seven when he died, but I've never got over him. I don't suppose I ever shall.'

'We imagine things,' Hunter said, out of the depth of his own experience. 'Especially we imagine happiness. It's always something past.'

She shook her head. 'Not this. It was real. Sometimes I think nothing since then has been real in the same way.'

'Then your mother married again.'

'Two years after Norman died, yes. Daddy was mad about her, went to the theatre every night, sent her flowers, took her out, all that sort of nonsense.'

'That must have been painful for you.'

'Oh, I didn't mind. I was only a kid, you know, I thought it was funny, that's all. Norman brought home presents after he'd been away, but as for hanging round Mummy, taking her out, buying her jewellery and all that – well. It just struck me as funny. I suppose I judge everything by Norman.'

'But he was nice to you?'

'Who?'

'Your stepfather. Lord Moorhouse.'

'Oh, he was nice all right.' She bit a fingernail, spat. 'Too nice.'

'How do you mean?'

'Mummy died when I was thirteen, you know that, don't you? She had cancer of the stomach. I was sixteen when he made a pass at me.'

'Your stepfather?'

'Who else? He was a bit tight at the time, at least that was the excuse he made afterwards. I dare say it was true.'

'That's why you hate him.'

'Is it? I don't know. Do you have to have a reason for hating anybody? Or liking anybody? He's been pretty nice to me in some ways. I'm an awful bitch you know, you don't want to have anything to do with me really.'

He said nothing. She stood up. She was swaying slightly on her feet, although they had not had much to drink. 'Come on, let's go back to your old Cosmos. I'm sick of it here.'

Back in the room with the mauve wallpaper it was again an animal rather than a woman in his arms, a thing that fought and tore.

A little less than two weeks later, he suggested that they should get married.

She burst out laughing and then, immediately contrite, put a hand over his. 'I'm sorry. But it's impossible, don't you see? We've had terrible fun, we'll go on having it, but – why, Daddy would never let me.'

'I thought you did what you wanted to do.'

'I do, but...' she left the sentence unfinished. 'I do love you. You know that, don't you?'

'I don't know it,' he said sullenly. 'You're like a little girl play acting. When it comes to reality you get frightened and say "Oh, I didn't mean that."'

'It's not that I'm frightened. I don't think I'm afraid of anything. But don't you see...'

'No.'

'I'm trying to be honest. Don't you see, it's the kind of thing I don't want. I told you I can't ever forget Norman.'

He said incredulously, 'But you were seven when he died. You're nursing a fantasy about him, that's all.'

'I know all that. I know Norman wasn't – respectable. He wasn't a good man. Not in the way that you're good.'

'That's the first time anybody has called me good.'

She was impatient. 'I know you've been in prison and all that. I don't mean that. But don't you see, the way Norman lived is the way I want to live too. I'm like him, I'll never be anything else.'

'That's only an idea. And a pretty silly one.'

'Even if I did want to get married, it would be impossible for us. I want money, Bill, I want that more than anything. What should we live on?'

'We could live abroad. I've got some money. I could get a job.'

'How long would the money last? And when it had gone, what sort of job would you get? A clerk in an insurance office? Do you think I want to keep house for you in a two-roomed flat in Brussels or Barcelona while you go out to work every day? Christ, no.' He did not answer. She said tenderly, 'I'm no good. You ought to be able to see that by now. I really am no good to anybody, Bill. Especially I'm no good to you. We'd better stop seeing each other.'

'I don't know what you're like,' he said. 'I don't know what you want. I wish I did.'

'I don't know either. But I think I know what *you* want.' She had been sitting on the bed, cross-legged. Now she got off it and went over to the window, looking out on Wilton Road. 'It's fine. Let's go to Kew Gardens.'

They went to Kew, and for the rest of the afternoon she was more unaffectedly gay than he had ever known her. She left him, as usual, just after six o'clock. He rarely saw her in the evenings, and to his own surprise was able to accept without jealousy the idea that she saw Roger on the evenings when she did not go somewhere with her stepfather. On this day, however, there seemed some difference in her way of saying goodbye. He was suddenly alarmed, and in need of an assurance that he would see her again.

'Don't look like that,' she said. 'I'll ring up.'

'Shall I see you tomorrow?'

'No. I've got to go away.'

'Next week?'

'I don't know if I'll be back.'

'You don't want to see me again.' He struggled to keep some shreds of his self-respect, struggled not to plead openly. 'All right. If that's what you want.'

'For God's sake,' she said impatiently. 'You don't know what life's about, do you? It's not a matter of what I want.'

'What then?'

'I don't know. I can't explain. I just have to work things out.' Her voice was high, hysterical.

'Write to me.'

She shook her head. 'Never write letters. I'll ring, that's for sure. Have fun.' She kissed him on the cheek, and was gone.

Chapter Twelve

The gap left by her absence was enormous. He had known her for three weeks and during that time the whole context of his life seemed to have changed, so that the future which had been first bright and then blank, now seemed to have meaning only if it included her. He had woken in the morning with the knowledge that he would see her at some time that day, hear her light voice, with a hint of self-mockery in it, arranging a meeting. It was apparent to him that he could not live without her, and that by some means he must make it possible for them to live together.

He attended the trial of the twenty people arrested at the Dance Rooms. The manager went to prison for three months, the drummer got six months for being in possession of dangerous drugs – he had a packet containing hemp in his jacket – and several other people got small fines. Roger Sennett, who pleaded guilty to attempting to resist arrest, was fined fifty pounds, a sentence which he received without a change of expression on his dark, heavy face.

On the following day he read in *The Times*,

under the heading 'Today's Arrangements': 'Lord Moorhouse on "The Fellowship Circle and the Bond of Empire Unity," at Propert Hall. 3 o'clock.' He went after lunch to Propert Hall, a decaying piece of Victorian red brick just off the Gray's Inn Road. There was an audience of about fifty people, some old and redly Blimpish, others young and with an eager scoutmasterly air. Two old ladies and a rather familiar-looking figure of military appearance whispered on the platform. A yellow-faced middle-aged man with a prominent Adam's apple bobbed up and down urgently between platform and audience. Then Lord Moorhouse appeared.

It is often difficult to identify the reality of physical appearance with an original mental conception, and to Hunter, Lord Moorhouse came as a shock. He was not a modern Mr Barrett, large, fleshy and overbearing, but a mild, bright-eyed, birdlike, clean little old man, with very neat hands and feet. Could this be the man who had made what Anthea called a pass at her – a thing which she had never referred to again – and towards whom her feelings were so strangely ambivalent?

Introduced by the military figure, Brigadier Fanshawe, as a mastermind of industry, one of the most important cogs in the great wheel of Britain's prosperity, Lord Moorhouse modestly insisted on his unimportance as an individual, and said that he came there to speak that day in his much more important capacity as Chairman of the Patriotic Fellowship Circle. In that capacity he wanted to tell them something about the vital link the Circle could be between...

Hunter put his head back and found his eyes closing. He was suddenly bored with the thing, and wondered what he had hoped to find out by coming there. For three-quarters of an hour he half-consciously listened to the bright bird voice mouthing platitudes, then to the baying of Brigadier Fanshawe. There was a paper collection, for which several fivers were offered with apparent spontaneity, and then a silver collection round the hall, made by the man with the Adam's apple. Hunter dropped two shillings into the bag.

Afterwards he drank tea and ate Dundee cake and then, with the sense of an endless measure of time to kill, took a bus that dropped him near Cavendish Square, and walked through. When he was some twenty yards away from the steps, the door opened and two people came out. One was the man with the Adam's apple. The other was Anthea. The man carried an umbrella with which he feebly tried to engage the attention of passing taxis. Anthea saw Hunter, must have seen him, on the pavement. It seemed to him that she hesitated, uncertain whether or not to greet him. Then the Adam's apple man got a taxi and opened the door. She turned her back to Hunter, got into the taxi, and they drove away.

Chapter Thirteen

It was two days later that she telephoned him.

'Hallo, Mr Smith, are you angry with me?'

He said carefully, 'Why should I be angry because you don't acknowledge that I exist?'

'That means you are. Oh, dear. I was coming to see you this afternoon. That all right?'

'Yes.'

'Same time, same place. 'Bye.'

When she came up the stairs to his room that afternoon, he was shocked by her appearance. Her eyes blazed in a face on which the flesh seemed stretched tightly across the bones, and when they kissed she clung to him with an eagerness that seemed less love than desperation. Their lovemaking was brief, and after it she shook with sobs. Later, as they lay on the bed, she timidly touched his hand.

'You saw me outside the house.'

'You know I did.'

'And you want to know about it, why I didn't say hallo.'

'I don't need to ask why. You want to keep your life at home separate from the little affair you're having with an ex-convict. That's quite exciting in its way, but naturally I understand that Anthea Moorhouse doesn't want her respectable friends to know about it. There's nothing to explain.'

'You can't think that, you know it's not true. Oh, you are a fool.' She beat at him with her fists.

'I don't know any more what is true or what isn't. I only know what I see. You said you were going away.'

'That was a lie. Oh, Bill, I've made such a mess of my life.'

The absurdity of her saying that, a girl of twenty-three who had never been to prison, never endured the agony of isolation from her fellows, touched him.

'I've thought about it all, everything you said.'

'Yes.'

'And I've decided we've got to go on. That's what you want too, Bill, isn't it?'

'Get married, do you mean?'

The words tumbled eagerly out of her. 'I don't know about that, but I've got to get away from all this. Daddy and everything, I mean. You do want me to go away with you, Bill, don't you? Because I've thought of a way to do it.'

She was sitting up naked, cross-legged, her

face serious, tears smudged away. It seemed to him that he wanted nothing else.

'This is how,' she said, and told him.

He stared at her, unable to believe that she was serious. 'You're crazy,' he said at last.

She tapped the palm of one hand with the finger of another. 'I'm not crazy. First of all, we want to live abroad. Second, we must have money to live on. This is a safe way of getting it. Third, when we're abroad we really want to disappear. This way we could do it.'

'It's crazy,' he said again. 'We'd never get the money.'

'If we didn't, there'd be no harm done. But we would get it.'

'We might be found out.'

'My father would never prosecute. But if we do it properly we shan't be caught.'

'You're serious about this, aren't you?' he said wonderingly. 'You really do mean it.'

'I've never been more serious about anything. And if you want what you say you want, you'll be serious too.'

'You know I want it. But this – it just doesn't make sense.'

'All right.' She jumped off the bed and walked over to the clothes which, as always, she had flung on the floor. 'You've changed.'

'What do you mean?'

'Once you were willing to carry a gun and fire it. Now you don't have to carry a gun, but you're frightened. That's what I mean.'

'You don't know what you're talking about, you little fool.' He was suddenly frantically angry. He caught her and forced her, struggling, back on to the bed. She fought, for minutes as it seemed, scratching and biting, before she suddenly relaxed in his arms. Afterwards, looking at her on the bed, eyes closed, body limp, face drawn and pale, he was conscious both of tenderness and of need for her. 'Tell me about it again. Perhaps it's not so crazy.'

She opened her eyes. 'Not crazy at all. Simple. I disappear. We send a note saying I've been kidnapped. Another, telling Daddy the amount of ransom money. A third, saying how the money is to be delivered. We collect the money, go abroad. I don't see what could be simpler.'

'How much money?'

She bit her fingernail. 'Not sure what I'm worth to him. Say seventy-five thousand pounds.'

'Like winning the pools.' But the amount really seemed to take the thing away into fairyland. 'He'd never pay it. After all, you aren't his daughter.'

'Do you think that matters!' Her laughter had as little humour as a dog's bark. 'You don't value me very highly, do you? All right, sixty thousand. Not a penny less.'

'He'll go to the police. He'll give us paper

wrapped in a bundle, instead of notes.'

She spat out a bit of nail. 'I don't think he'll go to the police. He wants me, you know. I'm his most valuable possession, better even than his collection of Waterford glass. I don't mean because of what I told you but he just does want me, that's all. We'll make it clear that if he goes to the police–' She drew a hand across her throat and rolled her eyes. 'I don't think he'll do it then. And for the same reason I don't think he'll give us paper instead of cash.'

'And if you're wrong?'

'That's the risk. But if we're caught I'll take the responsibility, say I planned it. Quite true, too. Do you think Lord Moorhouse is going to prosecute his stepdaughter for trying to get money out of him? What a disgrace for a man trying to forget his own lowly origins.'

'Don't you have any feelings about him at all?'

'I hate him,' she said, and would not look at Hunter.

'Assume he does get the police on to the ransom notes. How are we going to arrange for him to deliver the money without being caught ourselves?'

'That's what we have to work out, master criminal. If you ask me, it'll be fun doing it. And we're on sixty thousand pounds to nothing. Still think it's crazy?'

'Yes,' he said, but more doubtfully. 'There are so many things to think of – a hiding place for you, the ransom notes, the delivery of the money, getting away. A slip up on just one of them and–' He stopped. He had been talking as if he was going to do it.

'That's just what's fun, thinking about them.' She jumped off the bed again, and began hurriedly to put on her clothes. 'Come on,' she said. 'Let's go to one of those places you like. Let's go to the Tower of London. And think.'

Chapter Fourteen

That was the beginning of the plot, the kidnap plot, to which up to the end he never acknowledged himself committed. It would be fun, he agreed with Anthea, at least to talk about the plot and see how nearly foolproof they could make it, but with his agreement went the mental reservation that this was, after all, only talk. He told himself that he put it in the same category as speculations about what one would do after winning the pools.

From the first Anthea was so dazzled by the brilliance of the idea that she lacked much interest in working out its execution. It would be enough, she thought, for her to disappear, taking a train to some little place in Devon or Cornwall and staying there for a few days until the ransom money was paid. But he refused even to consider this, and they spent hours in arguing about the need for and possibility of disguise, the planting of false trails and the leaving of some misleading message. When she had accepted the idea that a simple disappearance would not be enough, Anthea was inclined to over-elaborate, and wanted to leave a note in her bedroom, saying that she was being forced to leave by a masked man, and a subsequent note written in her own blood, to be posted presumably by a friendly jailer.

All such ideas he vetoed. All that was necessary in the way of disguise, he thought, was that she should screw her hair up in a bun at the back of her head and wear a pair of glasses, but he was reluctant to let her register at a seaside hotel as a casual visitor, for fear that somehow she would reveal her identity. He was reluctant, also, to let her go abroad before the money had been paid, because a single woman passenger might engage notice. The essential thing, he insisted, was a place in which she could stay for anything up to a week without being seen. Really without being seen – that meant, with no possibility of being spotted by some busybody who informed the police.

They talked about it for a long time without result until suddenly, one day, she snapped her fingers.

'I've got it. The den.'

She went on to explain that her stepfather owned some three hundred acres of land, adjacent to Bassington Old Manor. Most of it was pasture, but there were a few acres of woods and in these woods was tucked the ruined little old stone shack which she called the den.

He was doubtful about it. 'It's on his estate. I don't like that. Then what about gamekeepers? Poachers? Or just tramps?'

Nobody ever came near it, she insisted, and the fact that it was on her father's estate was a positive advantage. All she had to do was to get in a stock of provisions, with a little primus and a sleeping bag, and hole up there for a week, which would be fun. Nothing could be simpler.

He was not persuaded at the time, but when they paid a visit to the den he saw what she meant. They got off at Blanting, a small railway junction, turned off the road outside the village, and walked three miles over fields without meeting anybody. Then they got under some barbed wire, and she told him they were now on the estate. She led the way with certainty over paths that seemed almost invisible to him, until they came to a dense, dark wood of poplars. Now she led him on for another few minutes until they came to a small glade.

'Here we are.'

He looked round. There was nothing to be seen all round but the poplars. There was one overgrown path that seemed to lead on through the wood. Otherwise, nothing.

'I don't see anything.'

'You're not meant to.' She pointed towards a spot where the undergrowth was most thickly tangled, and began resolutely to push a way through it. Hunter rather gingerly followed, protecting his face against brambles which clung like hands to his tweed jacket. The house, invisible until you reached it, was within a few yards of where they had been standing. House was a grandiose name for the place, yet it was more than a hut, a brick-built structure with a sound stone roof. The one small window was broken, the thick wooden door creaked as they opened it, and the one room contained a rickety table and a chair. There was no fireplace.

Anthea looked round with delight. 'Haven't been here for, oh, ten years, but it looks just the same. Nobody knows about it. Don't you think it's the most marvellous secret place? Terrific fun.'

He agreed that it was. 'Supposing a tramp–'

'I tell you *nobody* comes here. You can see that. Look at the dust.'

'And you wouldn't mind being here for five days?'

'Of course not. It would be fun.'

'What about water?'

'There's a little spring a few yards away in the wood.'

'Supposing you're seen coming here–'

'If I meet anyone on the way from Blanting here I telephone you, we call it off, and try again later, I mean anyone who might even possibly recognise me.'

'Anyone at all,' he said firmly. She looked at him, and he laughed uneasily. 'I agree it's an ideal place – that is, it would be if we were going to do it.'

So the place was settled. Then the ransom notes. They agreed that there was an element of risk in using a typewriter, and that the notes should be made up from old newspapers, stuck on ordinary thin bank paper. They bought all the daily newspapers for two days and then began to make up the notes from them, wearing rubber gloves and sticking down the letters with gum. Making up the words proved to be a laborious process, with which Anthea got very bored, but at last two letters were done. They did not do the third, because they had not worked out a plan for collection of the money.

About the amount of money itself they argued violently. Hunter insisted that sixty thousand pounds was still far too much, and also increased immensely the danger that her father would go to the police. If they were modest, and asked for ten thousand, he suggested, they would greatly diminish the risk. Anthea appeared to regard the mention of such a sum almost as an insult to her. Reluctantly she agreed at last to an amount of thirty thousand pounds. For Hunter, this was a sum that still left the plot in the region of fantasy. He had never had in his possession a tenth of thirty thousand pounds.

It was still no more than a game. They had done nothing decisive, as he told himself again and again. Yet he knew that, although this was literally true, he was emotionally more deeply committed with every hour of argument, every new speculation about the way in which the ransom should be collected. Anthea regarded the kidnap plot as settled, and thought him tediously slow and cautious.

Her ideas about collecting the money were not subtle. She suggested that they should instruct her father to leave it in a specific place, a certain garbage tin somewhere in the suburbs, say, and that they should then pick it up. She was convinced that he would not approach the police, and that they were therefore perfectly safe. Hunter did not share this conviction, and in any case wanted a plan that would be as far as possible foolproof. It took him three days to work out something with which he was reasonably satisfied, and another day to test it in company with Anthea, who played the role allotted to her stepfather. He felt a sort of pure intellectual pleasure that the plan worked well. She rather impatiently admitted that there seemed to be nothing wrong with it.

At this time they were seeing each other every day, in the mornings and afternoons as well. In the evenings, she said, her stepfather expected to know what she was doing, and he accepted this explanation, although he felt that she probably went out quite often with Roger Sennett. She had suddenly become bored with the Cosmos, and some of his dreams about her were made into a distorted reality. They went to Hampton Court, Battersea Fun Fair, took out a boat at Richmond, but it was not as he had imagined it, because they talked of nothing but the kidnap plot. They were now, indeed, less like lovers than like slightly quarrelsome partners in a business enterprise. As a partner, he felt some doubts of her.

'You're sure nobody – your father or anybody else –knows where you go to in the daytime?'

'Of course not. I told you I lead my own life, have my own friends. Daddy doesn't try to interfere as long as I don't get into trouble.'

'What sort of trouble?'

'Oh, you know. Like that time at the Dance Rooms. If I'd been arrested like Roger, he'd have made a fuss.'

It seemed to him that there was something evasive about her answer. 'You're quite sure you've not told anybody, anybody at all, about me?'

'Oh, for God's sake,' she said irritably, 'don't be so–'

'So what?'

'Nothing.' She kissed him. 'But tell me. Are we going to do it or not?'

They were in a boat on the river, just below Richmond Bridge. She wore a white sleeveless frock that made her look cool, beautiful, young, and infinitely desirable. What are you hesitating for, he asked himself, you're a lucky man.

'Yes,' he said. 'We're going to do it.'

Chapter Fifteen

Now that it was decided – although, as he continually reminded himself, he still retained the possibility of choice – he rang up Charlie Cash.

Charlie seemed pleased to hear from him. 'Bill, boy. How's tricks?'

'All right. Charlie, do you remember talking to me a few weeks ago about currency fiddlers, saying it might be an idea to build a programme round one?'

'I remember. But there isn't a hope in hell of your doing that now, Bill.'

'I know that. I've got an idea for a couple of newspaper articles that I might sell. What do you think?'

'I suppose you might.' Charlie did not sound encouraging.

'You said at the time that you could get me an introduction to a couple of them.'

'That's right. Westmark and Dawes.'

'Can you do that?'

'Nothing easier. But I honestly don't see what you'll get out of it. These are tough boys, you know. They play around with other things besides currency fiddling. It was a pretty crummy idea in the first place.'

'Let me worry about that. If you can arrange for me to see one of them, Charlie, I'll appreciate it. The name's Smith, Bill Smith, and just say it's a business deal, nothing more than that.'

'What are you up to, Bill?'

'I told you, I may be able to write a couple of articles.'

'I know what you told me. It's no skin off my nose, but I don't like the sound of it. I'll give you Westmark's telephone number, that's Theo Westmark. It's an ex-directory number. You can say you got it from me. That's as far as my name will take you. If you don't have any luck with Westmark, try Dawes. I'll give you his number too.'

He took down the numbers. 'Thank you, Charlie. That's a great help.'

'You're welcome.' There was curtness, less in the words than in the way they were spoken.

Theo Westmark lived in a penthouse at the top of a small block of flats in Park Lane. There were gilt cupids in the lift, and three of its sides were covered with striped wall-paper. A Chinese girl opened the door of the flat. Her face was a cosmetic mask. The shape of her lips was completely obscured by a thick mass of lipstick formed into a huge, grotesque cupid's bow. The effect was rather as though a moustache had been scrawled on to the photograph of a film star. The girl wore a long coat embroidered with what seemed to be some sort of shining stones. It was cut away at top and bottom like a morning coat, to reveal her breasts and thighs.

The girl murmured something, and left him, Inside the flat there was a rich, warm smell. Hunter felt as though he were inside a particularly spicy fruit cake. The little hall he stood in was dimly lighted by indirect shades on the walls. They illuminated, more than anything else, several pornographic drawings.

The Chinese girl came back and murmured again. Hunter followed her down a dimly-lighted corridor with more drawings on the walls. He walked through an open door into a huge room flooded with light. This room was furnished with elegant chairs and spindly sofas, all covered with striped brocade. There were several small, finicky, perfectly respectable paintings. China ornaments, shepherdesses and milkmaids, stood on shelves. One wall of the room was a great sheet of glass, a vast window overlooking the Park.

The man who came to meet him was big, fleshy, smiling. His smooth face was tanned and healthy, his air relaxed. He wore a silk shirt of pale lemon yellow, and a dark grey tie with a large ruby pin. His cuff-links were diamonds, his suit a very pale grey.

'Mr Smith? That is a good anonymous name – yet where will one find a name more probable? You will drink a glass of Madeira with me.' Westmark poured two glasses of rosy wine from a crystal decanter. 'This is not ordinary Madeira. It has an interesting history. The wine was bottled in 1803, and for something like a hundred years lay in the cellars of the Earl of Clarnish. The Earl, a man unaware of what constitutes the good life, did not touch it. His son was alive to its virtues, but was also – what shall I say? – upon occasion, indiscreet. I was able to assist him in one or two small matters, and this was part of my reward. A reward not beyond price, perhaps, but one I value more than quite a sizeable cheque.'

The wine was rich and sweet, and held for Hunter a reminiscence of the smell that seemed to pervade the flat. Westmark drank it greedily, and poured another glass. He went on talking about various members of the aristocracy whom he had been able to help, about the ways in which they had repaid him, all with a kind of vague grandiloquence that Hunter found disagreeable.

'The good life,' Westmark said meditatively, 'it is what we all want, is it not, Mr Smith? For the fakir his bed of nails, a strange pleasure that I can never understand. For young Landing, about whom I have been telling you, the thrill of putting more money than he can afford on the fall of a card. For me wine – not any wine, but one like this Madeira that has age and prestige, history in its colour and smell. And women – not any women, but those like my Chinese kitten, who have been trained to obedience. For each of us something different.'

He's a show off, Hunter thought contemptuously, he likes to talk. Aloud he said, 'I came to talk about a currency deal.'

Now Westmark's loquacity disappeared, as a conjurer's patter is changed for action. 'How much, and to what country?'

'It would be quite a lot of money.'

'How much?'

'About thirty thousand pounds.'

Westmark showed no surprise. He was looking at his Madeira, turning the glass round and round.

Hunter continued. 'The country is not important. Somewhere in Europe, Italy, Switzerland, Spain. It doesn't matter.'

Westmark nodded his large head. 'That can be arranged.'

'How?'

'You pay me the money. A banking account is opened for Mr William Smith in Zurich, say, or Berne, or Genoa, by my agents. They will pay the money into the account to await your collection. My charge is modest, no more than five per cent.'

Hunter shook his head. 'I don't want a banking account. It can cause complications.'

'Very well. Then you go direct to an agent, and he will pay you the money. Is that what you want?'

'Yes. But I have to trust you. I want some proof that I'm safe in doing that.'

'What sort of proof do you expect, what proof can I give you? You can speak to anybody who knows me, and ask if Theo Westmark is to be trusted.' The big man was watching Hunter carefully. 'I have been trusted not for thousands of pounds, but for a quarter of a million. But trust is not necessary. A property can be bought for you, an account can be opened on which your own agent can draw the very day your cheque here is cashed. If you do not wish to use such an agent, if you want to receive the cash from my own representative, then – you must trust me.' Westmark's voice was soft as he said, 'Mutual trust is the basis of business dealings, Mr Smith. You are not trusting me very far when you do not tell me your name.'

He had no agent abroad whom he could trust. Nor was it a cheque that he would hand over to Westmark, but cash. Once the money was in Westmark's hands he could in any case cheat Hunter if he wanted to do so. On the other hand, Westmark had no means of knowing that Hunter would not return to England. All this passed through his mind while he said, 'My name is Smith.'

Westmark shrugged.

'I trust you. But I ought to add that I have friends here who will look after my interests.'

Westmark said gently, 'Mutual trust should exclude threats, Mr Smith. Come to me when you are ready. You will always find me here, with my Madeira and my kitten.'

The taste of Madeira was in Hunter's mouth, and the spicy fruit cake smell strong in his nostrils as he left the flat.

Chapter Sixteen

On the following day he had discovered a flaw in their plans, a flaw of such dimensions that it made him doubt the whole conception. If they could fail to notice such a mistake as this, perhaps another error, equally vast, was yawning elsewhere in the plot. This was the flaw. When they left the country after collecting the money, Anthea would have to show her passport. Obviously they could not run the considerable risk that a customs official would recognise her photograph or remember her name.

When he told Anthea the problem, she said scornfully, 'But it's simple.'

'What do you mean?'

'We just go on one of those day trips, Boulogne or wherever it is, the trips on which you don't need passports. Then we skip off at Boulogne and just vanish.'

'No,' he said decisively. 'You don't understand. There's going to be a hell of a fuss about your disappearance, even if your father doesn't eventually tell the police. Anything out of the way is going to be checked. Two people vanishing off a day trip – not just missing the boat and coming back next day, but disappearing altogether – is something out of the way. Who were the people, what did they look like? Once they've got that far, it's goodbye.'

'I don't see why you say that. Daddy would never prosecute.'

'It's no good.'

'We could move from place to place, so that they didn't catch up with us. We'd have enough money.'

'No.'

They were in the hotel bedroom. She sat gloomily contemplating her legs, which were stuck out in front of her. 'That's it, then.'

'How do you mean?'

'You don't want to take the risk. I expect you're right. So the whole thing's no good.'

It was very much what he had been about to say himself, but that she should say it was disconcerting. It was rather as though she were saying goodbye, not merely to the kidnap plot but to him as well. He was driven to words he had not at all intended. 'It may not be as bad as that.'

'Why not?'

'We might think of something,' he said weakly. But her imagination, which was so quickly damped, just as quickly caught alight again. 'Do you mean you could do something about it? Get mine altered – or get another?'

That was precisely, he knew, what he could do, although it was an idea that he had not previously allowed himself to consider. Ten years in prison had left him with a great deal of knowledge which he never used – where to get a burglar's kit, which fences handled which kinds of stuff. Like most men who have done a long stretch he had also developed a special sensibility to stool pigeons. He knew that false passports could be obtained, at something between twenty and fifty pounds a time, and he could easily find out where to get them. But he did not want to admit this knowledge. Certainly he did not want to use it.

'I suppose I could see a few people. Or we might think of something else.'

She ignored the second sentence. 'That would be marvellous. Could I come too?'

'Certainly not. But we shall need a passport photograph. You'd better get one taken.'

'What fun? She looked at his gloomy face, 'Isn't it fun?'

'No. It's just something that has to be done. Don't think that I like doing it.'

'Poor Bill. But I'll make it up to you. It will be all right when it's over and we're abroad, you'll see. You do like our plot, don't you, you think it's clever?' She was like a child, eager for admiration.

'The plot's clever, all right. It's just that

when we come to do it–' He left the sentence unfinished. He could not say that he distrusted himself and, even more, distrusted her.

She went away chirruping like a bird, and came back next day still chirruping. When she gave him the photographs he could not refrain from laughing with her. A formidable Germanic schoolmistress confronted him, hair scraped back from her forehead and screwed into a bun, eyes staring grimly through ornamental spectacles. She took the spectacles out of her bag, blue ones with much-jewelled sides, and put them on.

'Don't I look just wonderful? What's my name, do you think? Jane something? Or Mary, I think this girl's a real good old Mary, don't you? I suppose Ethel would be a bit too much, wouldn't it? Aren't you pleased with me for thinking of the spectacles.'

'Very pleased.' As he kissed her, he wondered what else he had forgotten.

On the next day he looked up a man named Leafy Cockerell, who had been in prison with him, and was now manager of a club in Soho. He gave Leafy two pounds, and Leafy sent him along with a note to a little tailor's shop off the Mile End Road. In a room at the back of the shop sat an old man. He wore a thick padded red coat, with gold brocade at the collars and cuffs. A large green eyeshade concealed his face.

'You want a book, eh? You have a picture.' Hunter gave him the photograph of the Germanic schoolmistress. He barely glanced at it. 'Just this one. Nothing for yourself?'

'Nothing.' It was possible, though not likely, that an official might recognise him. To change the name on his passport would be merely an additional risk.

The old man's face, when he raised it to look at Hunter, was criss-crossed like the road map of an industrial area. In the map the eyes were hardly visible, their colour and expression unknown. 'I do a lovely job.' He handed over a passport with gold and blue cover, crisp and new. Hunter examined it with admiration, holding up the pages to the light for the watermark.

'Very expensive, that paper,' the old man said. 'Fifty pounds.'

Hunter put down the passport, shook his head. 'Impossible.'

'This is no rubbish. The real stuff. You want to get the girl out of the country.'

'It is too much, more than I can afford. Twenty.' The old man tucked his hands in the sleeves of the padded coat. 'Ridiculous. You are joking with me. It costs me more than that.'

The haggling process was familiar to Hunter. They settled, as he had expected, at thirty-five.

When he left the tailor's shop he felt that

he had done something irrevocable. He noted with wry distaste that his association with Anthea was leading, as he had expected, back into the past.

Three days later he gave her the passport. It was made out in the name of Mary Nash, spinster, of 18 Novella Road, NW2. She took it from him, exclamatory with pleasure.

'It's lovely, isn't it? So much more exciting than a real one.'

'It's real enough to serve. At least, I hope so.'

'Now there's nothing to stop us.'

'Nothing.'

'So the sooner the better. Today's Saturday. On Monday I'll disappear. You send the first note that day. You should have the money by Thursday.'

'Thursday, or Friday at the latest. You remember what we arranged.'

'Yes. I'm to wait till Saturday.' She ran the tips of her fingers softly over his cheek. They kissed passionlessly, their lips just brushing each other. 'Good luck. Not that you'll need it.'

'Goodbye.'

'Goodbye.'

Chapter Seventeen

On Sunday Anthea was to mention casually, to her father, to Roger Sennett, to anybody else with whom she happened to be in conversation, that a tall man with a slight limp was following her. Hunter had finally agreed, rather reluctantly, to the laying of this false trail. He had a feeling that she would be inclined to overdramatise the story in a way that would arouse suspicion. She had made an appointment to go shopping on Monday morning with a friend named Mary Winter. Early that day she was to telephone this friend, say that she would be along at eleven o'clock, and express vague uneasiness about her own affairs, referring again to the man with the limp.

She would not arrive at Mary Winter's flat. Instead, she was to change her hairstyle, put on the spectacles, buy provisions, sleeping bag and other equipment, and stuff them into a rucksack. Then she was to take a train to Blanting and, an inconspicuous girl hiker with rucksack on back, make her way to the den. It was understood that she and Hunter would have no communication after that time until the money was collected.

As soon as he got the money he was to book air passages for them both to almost any European country. Anthea had been in favour of making three separate advance bookings for Thursday, Friday and Saturday, but he had rejected this idea on the ground that the necessary cancellation of two bookings might arouse suspicion. Once abroad, in Italy or Yugoslavia or Greece or Northern Africa, with thirty thousand pounds, they would – but his imagination never reached that point, it was set too firmly on what lay immediately ahead.

After making the air booking he was to go down to the den and collect Anthea. If she had heard nothing by Saturday she was to leave the den and telephone him. If the plot had somehow gone wrong she was to return home and pretend to have suffered loss of memory, so that she knew nothing of her own movements during the past few days. That was the plan, one that, she maintained, covered every possible contingency.

Nevertheless, it was with a sinking heart that, on Monday, he began to carry it out. It was less that he was afraid than that he still could not believe in the plan's reality. If, on Monday morning, he telephoned Cavendish Square and asked for Miss Moorhouse, surely she would answer, would say in her light voice, 'Oh, *that*, I didn't suppose you'd really take that seriously, of course it was tremendous fun to plan but you didn't *really* suppose that I'd do it...'

He must not telephone, he told himself. He must not permit himself to think like that. Wearing gloves, he sent off the first ransom note by the midday post on Monday. The cut-out letters stuck on thin copy paper said:

This is to tell you that we have got your daughter. Do not inform the police and she will not be harmed. Await instructions.

The comparatively mild tone of this note had been achieved at his insistence. Anthea had been in favour of something much more bloodthirsty and threatening, signed 'The Black Devils; or something like that. But Hunter was convinced that the first letter should be quiet, almost reassuring in tone. It would be sufficient indication that they meant business to enclose with the letter one of her small pearl earrings.

He had expected that after putting the letter in the box he would feel somehow a different man, one engaged upon a criminal enterprise. In fact he was conscious of nothing except the vast expanse of time that yawned between the present moment and his next sight of Anthea. Monday, Tuesday, Wednesday, how were they to be filled? He sat for an hour in an Espresso coffee bar, ate a lunch which he hardly tasted, went to the cinema and sat through a film which he barely saw. Afterwards he went back to the Cosmos, lay on his bed and stared up at the crack in the ceiling. The bed squeaked under him and he thought of that evening which seemed so long ago, although it was a period of time to be counted in weeks, when she had first come here. As he conjured up various pictures of her, sitting cross-legged on the bed, taking off her dress, making love, a creature incomprehensibly gay and then just as incomprehensibly gloomy, it occurred to him that, whether or not things went as they had planned, she would never come to the Cosmos again. The thought made him miserable. It seemed to him that he was like a man suspended between two lives, the past with Anna which he had given up, and the future with Anthea in which he could not really believe.

That evening he was jarringly reminded of the past. At half-past seven he decided that he could not bear to eat dinner in the Cosmos. Outside in Wilton Road a light rain was falling. He put on a raincoat and went down the stairs. A man had taken refuge from the rain in the entrance, Hunter made to push past him, the man turned, and revealed the red slightly sweating face (or were those really drops of rain?) of Jerry Wilton.

'Bill,' Jerry said. Hunter could see Jerry summing up the situation with one quick glance back into the hotel, a sharp look at Bill himself – is he keeping a little piece here or just economising? – and then the words coming fluently. 'Bill, you old son of a gun. This is a bit of luck. Let's go and have a drink.'

He allowed himself to be led by Jerry to the nearest pub, drank the beer that was bought for him, bought a beer back, talked warily of trivialities. Did it matter at all that Jerry Wilton connected him with the Cosmos, could it in any way affect the kidnap plot? He decided that it could not, and yet remained uneasy, aware of something more than usually false in Jerry's professional geniality. Leave it to Jerry, he told himself, he'll say what it's all about if and when he wants to. Jerry now was telling him how damned sorry he, Jerry, was that things had turned out the way they had.

'I want you to know that, Bill. I want you to know that you did a hell of a good job, and it's a damned shame things had to turn out this way.'

'I saw what you said in the interview in the papers. Thanks, Jerry.'

'No thanks about it. I just told the truth.' Beads of sweat showed on Jerry's face, there could be no doubt about his sincerity. But did people really say this kind of thing,

Hunter wondered, and answered himself that evidently they did.

'If it rested with me you'd still be on the job, Bill. But you know what it is, we've got to consider the public.' Jerry's voice was appropriately hushed as he spoke the holy word.

'Naturally. I understand that.'

'It wasn't good publicity for anybody.'

'No, of course not.'

'But I still think you had a raw deal. They could have found you another job, out of the public eye you might say. I've told everyone what I think about it. It's not often I stick my neck out, either.' Brave Jerry, Hunter thought, don't-hit-a-man-when-he's-down Jerry. But he could not help reflecting at the same time that Jerry had not stuck his neck out very far. His own resignation was an accomplished fact, the money acknowledging it was lodged in the bank, Jerry's defence of him was all glory and no danger. Was this too cynical a thought? Perhaps it was.

Yet in spite of the tears in Jerry's voice, surely this was not all he had to say? Still tearful, he added now, 'What's happened to you, Bill?'

'How do you mean?'

'You and the little woman, You're not together any more. That's a hell of a thing to happen. She's a great little woman, Bill.'

So it was Anna! After Charlie's reproaches came Jerry Wilton's tears. He could hardly refrain from laughing at the thought of Jerry, with his icily respectable wife, his house at Sunningdale, his two boys at good public schools, worrying about the cutting of his illegal bond with Anna. But it would never do to laugh. Pie-faced as Jerry himself, he said, 'It was the best way.'

Jerry shook his head. 'I feel a bit responsible. Do you know what I'd like to see? I'd like to see you marry that girl.'

Still playing the part expected of him, yet in a way telling the truth as well, he said, 'Sometimes you have to make a clean break. How could I ask Anna to marry me?'

'With the shadow hanging over you, you mean?' Jerry pushed another beer towards him. 'Yet, do you know, I believe Anna would have done it. Your feelings do you credit, Bill, but still I can't approve of the way you did it. She really took one on the chin when you just up and left her like that, but she hasn't let it floor her. At the same time I don't mind admitting, I'm worried about that girl, Bill.' Jerry looked deep into the mystical depths of his glass. 'And about you, too. That place tonight–' He shook his head.

Suddenly he was sickened by the pie-faced part, it was all more than he could stand, the boozy false sincerity of Jerry Wilton, who had dealt in lies so long that he could no longer tell them from the truth, the idealisation of placid, sluttish Anna, the whole deep mess of sentiment in which Jerry wanted to embed him. He put down his glass on the counter so that a little liquid slopped over the side. 'Shut up.'

'Don't think I'm trying to interfere, old man.'

'Oh, for Christ's sake.' He lifted his glass, let the beer roll down his throat, and spoke with a conscious effort at control. 'Let me alone, will you, Jerry.'

Jerry wiped his face. He looked surprised, a little frightened even. 'I'm sorry as hell you take it like that, Bill. Believe me, I didn't mean to offend you. If I've said anything out of turn, I'm sorry.'

'It's all right. I just want to be left alone.' Less out of interest than to change the subject, he said, 'Did you hear any more of Mekles? Threats to sue you, anything like that?'

'Nothing. But the police – my word, we had the police round asking questions every day for a week. I must say, Bill, I think you were rather – foolhardy, shall I say?'

'What do you mean?'

'Why, you saw the news of Bond's suicide in the paper and tried to link it to Mekles. Isn't that right?'

'I didn't know anything about Bond's

suicide,' he said patiently. It would be impossible to convince Jerry of that, as it had been impossible to convince Inspector Crambo. 'If it was suicide.'

'What do you mean?'

'Nothing.' There was no point in telling Jerry about what now seemed that rather ridiculous interview with Tanya Broderick. 'Will you believe it, Jerry, if I tell you that the only thing I knew about Bond was from the stuff Charlie supplied to me? He told me not to use it, but I did. I played a hunch and it went wrong, that's all.'

'Do you see any green?' Jerry rolled up the corner of an eyelid and revealed the bloodshot egg of his eye.

'No, it was a daring move, would have been a real scoop if it had come off and you'd rattled Mekles. I think it was foolhardy, but I respect you for trying it. I shall always think of you, Bill, as one of the most daring chaps I've ever known.'

It sounded valedictory. What would he call me, Hunter wondered, if he knew about the kidnap plot? That night he dreamed, not of Anthea but of Anna. There was a secret that she was for some reason prevented from telling him, and it was immensely important to them both that he should know it. What was the secret. 'Don't do it,' Anna said to him. 'It will bring you bad luck for seven years.' What was he not to do, he asked her frantically? She did not answer, merely shook her head and bit into a liqueur chocolate. Drops of the liquid dribbled down her chin.

Chapter Eighteen

On the following morning, Tuesday morning, he decided quite suddenly that he could not adhere to the timetable agreed with Anthea. According to this timetable he should have sent off that morning the second ransom note, telling Lord Moorhouse to draw thirty thousand pounds out of the bank, and threatening to kill Anthea if he informed the police. Then on Wednesday morning he was to telephone and instruct Moorhouse about delivery of the money.

But why, he asked himself, should he wait until Wednesday, why not telephone Moorhouse this morning, and get things moving? He knew the answer to this argument. The second letter would put Moorhouse really on the rack, and the extra twenty-four hours would soften him up so that he would be ready to pay up without question. He appreciated the force of this argument, but found himself disinclined – or should he say unable? – to regard it. The meeting with Jerry Wilton, harmless and obviously coincidental as it had been, had upset him, and at breakfast time on Tuesday something else happened, something by no means so trivial, which sealed his resolution.

The dining room at the Cosmos, which had sometimes a spurious gaiety about it at night, was a mausoleum in the morning. The only people who ever came down to breakfast were a very old Russian exile with a long white beard stained yellow round the mouth by nicotine, and an elegant young Indian homosexual, who said that he was doing research for a book about the changes in English social habits during the last ten years but, Hunter suspected, stayed in the Cosmos because he could bring back his friends there without any uncomfortable questions. A nod passed for greeting to them, and then Hunter sat down to his breakfast of coffee and cold, slightly soggy toast and marmalade.

Usually the waiter on in the mornings was Alphonse, who had some kind of ague so that his approach was always signified by a rattling of plates and cups which, miraculously, never fell to the floor. Today, however, the other waiter, Bert, was on duty. Bert was a Cockney with slickly brushed black hair, a snub nose, and merry little dark eyes. He brushed crumbs off the table, a few on to Hunter's clothes, poured his coffee, slid the marmalade off the tray on to the table, with a casual grace that was somehow insulting. Then he stood by the table and murmured something which Hunter, occupied with looking in the morning paper to see if there was anything about Anthea's disappearance, did not properly hear. There was nothing in the paper. It was hardly possible that there could be anything.

'What was that?' he asked.

'I said, shall we have the pleasure of seeing Miss Anthea today?'

For a moment Hunter was incapable of movement. His knife, engaged in buttering a piece of toast, stayed still, the hand holding the knife gripping it almost convulsively. He stared at the paper in front of him, on which the print had suddenly become unreadable. He was surprised by the calmness of his own voice as he said, 'What's that?'

Now he looked up at Bert's face, on which the characteristic knowing look had changed to a triumphant smirk. The waiter went across to one corner of the room and came back with an old, dog-eared *Tatler*. With a clean, neatly-trimmed nail he pointed to a picture at the bottom right-hand corner of one page. It showed Anthea in riding clothes, smiling and looking very fresh and young. Roger Sennett stood glowering by her side. The caption said, 'Glamorous Miss Anthea Moorhouse and the Honourable Roger Sennett enjoy a joke at a meeting of the East Hampshires near Alresford.'

'I thought you'd be interested,' Bert said. 'Seeing you and the lady are such friends.'

Hunter admired his own composure. 'I don't know what you're talking about. Am I supposed to know who this is?'

'Oh, come off it,' Bert said, but his voice was uncertain. Hunter gathered strength from it.

'Look here, young man,' he said, 'What are you trying to do?'

'Just thought you'd be interested. Wondered what her dad would think if he knew she came to see you at the old Cosmos, that's all.'

'I've never seen this girl before. Do you understand that?'

'If you say so.'

Hunter tapped the photograph with his finger. 'But if I had – *if* I had – it would be very silly of you to try to blackmail me about it. Was that what you had in mind?' He stared, directly and unflinchingly, at Bert. Under his hard gaze – or was it simply the use of the word *blackmail* – the young waiter shifted uncomfortably.

'Course not, Mr Smith. Just thought you'd be interested, that's all.' A little more confidently he went on, 'You got to admit she looks like–'

'I don't admit anything,' Hunter said sharply. 'And I should advise you to keep your mouth shut. Anything else would be silly. It might even be dangerous.'

'How do you mean?'

'I mean this. Don't think I'd hesitate to go to the police if you tried any funny business. That's all.' He dismissively returned to the paper, and to his coffee and toast.

Upstairs afterwards in his room he tried to assess the damage. He had shared, more or less, Anthea's certainty that no one could link them together – and now here was the link firmly established. What a curse it is, he thought, that the would-be criminal classes read the *Tatler*. And how comic it was that Bert should have recognised Anthea, but not Hunter himself, whose photograph had recently been in the national press.

Bert would not be scared for long. Within a couple of days he would have returned to the attack. And when the time came, when the plot had been carried out, and Anthea had not returned, and the news of the kidnapping was in the papers, he would open his mouth and sing loud and strong. Hunter would then be identified as a suspect. By that time, to be sure, he and Anthea should be out of the country.

He assured himself that the incident did not matter, although he knew that it did. In fact, as he vaguely understood, he was no longer really capable of assessing accurately what did or what didn't matter. To falter now, to give up the plot, meant the end of his life with Anthea – a life which was as yet no more than a promise of beaches where the sand was finer and the sea bluer than it ever was in reality, of little towns where people were anonymous and the sun always shone. Was all that only a vision? Even so, it was impossible for him to give it up. He could imagine the contempt with which Anthea would hear him when he told her that the plan had proved too risky, that he had had to abandon it. The thought that his relationship with her might end was more than he could bear. And if he was not to give up then he must go on, and go on quickly.

At half-past ten that morning he was in a call box at Victoria Station. He took a handkerchief out of his pocket and held it in front of his mouth. He hoped that this would blur his voice while still leaving it audible. The solemn voice of a subordinate spoke to him and asked his business, when he pressed button A.

'Tell Lord Moorhouse that I wrote him a letter yesterday about his daughter.'

There was a pause. Then came a voice which he recognised as Moorhouse's. The voice said simply, 'Yes?'

The words came easily enough. 'You got my letter.'

The birdlike tones he remembered were impatient now, even autocratic. If there was alarm in the voice Hunter could not hear it. 'About my daughter. Yes, I did. Is this some sort of practical joke?'

He said slowly, 'It's not a joke. Have you informed the police?'

The voice snapped back at him. 'Certainly not. I regard the whole thing as a piece of nonsense.'

'Did you think the earring was nonsense?' He waited for a reply to that, but none came. 'You'd better take us seriously if you want to see your daughter again.'

'Of course I want to see her again, man. Get down to brass tacks.'

This reversal of the normal roles of kidnapper and victim had disconcerted Hunter. Now it angered him. He took away the handkerchief, and spoke loudly. 'Listen to me and don't interrupt. If you want to see her again, this is what you must do. Withdraw thirty thousand pounds from the bank today in one pound notes. You understand that, in one pound notes. Not new ones, and they mustn't run consecutively. Put the money in a zipping canvas bag. Then wait for further instructions. Someone will telephone you this evening. Is that clear?'

For the first time the birdlike tones were subdued. 'I understand, yes. But I'm not at all sure I can get that amount of money by tomorrow–'

'You'd better get it if you want to see her.'

‘What about my daughter – Anthea. Is she well?’

Deliberately he said, ‘Your daughter is well. So far she is unharmed. She will remain unharmed if you do as we say.’

Now Moorhouse’s voice unmistakably faltered. ‘You really mean it isn’t a practical joke? You’d tell me if it were a joke, you wouldn’t keep it up this long.’

‘It’s no joke of any sort,’ Hunter said. ‘Do as we say. Get out the money and wait for a message. One more thing. We are watching you. If you tell the police, we shall know. Then the deal will be off, and I wouldn’t like to say what will happen.’

He put down the receiver, stepped out of the telephone box, and walked with an apparent decisiveness but with actual lack of purpose, down Victoria Street, and left into the park.

He told himself that he had carried it off pretty well, but he felt shame and fear rather than self-satisfaction. To make Moorhouse’s tone change from autocratic disbelief to something like submissiveness had had a kind of pleasure in it, but the pleasure was a degraded one, Anthea had apparently been able to think of her stepfather simply as a machine from whom money might be extracted, but for Hunter he had become a man whose feelings were being brutally exploited. He found the act of exploitation much more unpleasant than he had expected.

Fear was mixed with the sense of shame. It was all very well for Anthea to say blithely that they were not committing a crime, but what was demanding money with menaces but a crime? And although she might be right in saying that her father would never prosecute his stepdaughter, what reason was there to suppose that he would be given similar immunity? Walking through the park, standing on the bridge and staring at the children dropping bread to ducks, he saw the jaws of a trap closing on him, a trap which he was operating himself.

Yet, as he had also realised earlier that day, it was impossible for him to stop what he was doing, without losing Anthea. He remembered words which he had read long ago, 'There is a point beyond which there is no turning back. This is the point that must be reached.' Hunter felt that he had reached it.

Chapter Nineteen

Hunter was a great reader of brass plates outside office buildings, a wonderer about the secrets hidden (as it seemed to him) behind such names as the National Strain

Removers Association, or the Council for the Commercial use of Inorganic Materials, or the League of Steady Walkers. Now, as he walked idly out of the park and turned into a street just off Lower Regent Street, he read the plates in the doorways of the solid Victorian buildings, and was stopped by one particularly shining and beautiful and, to judge by its unscratched nature, new, that said PFC, 1st Floor. In smaller capitals, which descended finally to upper and lower case, the plate said PATRIOTIC FELLOWSHIP CIRCLE for Preserving the Bonds of Empire. He remembered the man with the Adam's apple, the moment outside the house when Anthea had looked at him without acknowledgement.

On the first floor there was a room that said 'Private', and another with a glass door lettered in black, 'Enquiries. Please Knock and Enter'.

He knocked and entered. A woman in her forties, with wisps of grey hair hanging down on either side of a red shapeless face, was busy at a typewriter. She looked up in a manner that he guessed was permanently flustered.

'Can I help you?'

'Perhaps you can. I wanted to find out something about the objects of the Fellowship.'

'Yes, yes. Just a moment. Now where–'

Her desk was littered with papers, and she began to search among them. The room was large, light, airy, the oak desk and steel filing cabinets looked new. Two doors led out of the room, both lettered in gold. On one the lettering said *Mr L G Rawlinson*, on the other *Mr H A Pine*.

The red-faced woman's search among the papers became a hen-like scrabbling. She brushed ineffectively at one of the wisps of hair, muttered, 'If you'll excuse me,' and went into Mr Rawlinson's room. When she came back the man with the Adam's apple was with her. He smiled at Hunter, showing a fine mouthful of false teeth.

'You wanted to know about the PFC, Mr – ah–'

'Smith.'

'I am the secretary of the Circle. Here is a little – ah – brochure, which sets out our primary aims and objects, the preservation and indeed – ah – strengthening of the bonds of Empire. We have monthly meetings at which all our friends are welcome. Inter-cultural exchange visits are paid. A young party came over from Rhodesia this year, and we shall be sending a group out there in the autumn.'

'A sort of Scout movement?' Hunter suggested. Mr Rawlinson gobbled. 'By no means. Have you any conception of the inroads made by international Communism in the Colonies? Few people have, I find. The PFC is combating the growth of Communism by sending out speakers to different parts of Empire, speakers who emphasise the Empire ideal. In this country we are carrying out a campaign, an – ah – *intensive* campaign, of circularisation. A selected list of *important* people has been chosen, and we are trying to make them aware of the extent of the danger. Would it surprise you to know that the Foreign Office is riddled with Communists, Mr Smith?'

'It would, yes.'

'Yet that is the case, I assure you. We have evidence to prove it.' A slight white foam showed on Mr Rawlinson's lips. He wiped it away with a handkerchief, and looked triumphantly at Hunter.

The door on the other side of the room opened and a thin, dark young man stood there, looking from one to the other of them. Rawlinson beamed.

'Arthur. We were just – ah – talking about the fine work the Circle was doing out in South Africa and Australia. This is Mr Pine, our – ah – Colonial organiser, who has been out to *both* countries this year, Mr – ah – Smith.'

The young man came forward smiling. He had an actor's voice, deep and melodious. 'You are interested in the Fellowship Circle, Mr Smith.'

'Yes.' Recklessly he said, 'A friend of mine named Anthea Moorhouse mentioned it to me.'

'Ah, yes.' Rawlinson nodded, pleased. 'She is one of our most *tireless* supporters, isn't she, Miss Framling?'

The middle-aged woman had been brooding over her typewriter. Thus appealed to, she nodded emphatically.

'I wish there were more like her, she is really wonderful. And her stepfather too – you know, he is our Chairman.'

'Yes. I heard him speak the other day. Anthea is an active worker for the Circle, then.'

'Did she tell you that?' There was an expression of puzzlement on Pine's thin, nervously handsome face.

'Yes, but she didn't say exactly what she did.'

'She helps Arthur mostly,' Rawlinson said. 'Another of his functions is that of raising funds, and she really has been *wonderfully* good about that. There are certain people whom we can always rely on for a monthly contribution if they are *personally* approached. She calls on them regularly, really never lets a month go by without seeing them.'

'I wonder if it would be possible for me to lend a hand with that kind of work,' Hunter said. 'If I joined, that is.'

One side of Pine's face moved slightly, in a nervous tic.

'Why, yes.' Rawlinson looked baffled. 'It's really Arthur's province but – ah – I feel sure there would be no objection. You are a friend of Miss Moorhouse's – of Anthea's.' Hunter nodded.

'There was something I wanted to see you about, Leslie,' Pine said abruptly. 'In connection with the group visit for New Zealand. It's rather urgent.'

'Oh, yes. Yes.' Rawlinson dabbed again at his lips, held out a hand. 'You'll read the brochure, Mr Smith, and let us know your feelings. Do let us know if there's any other – ah – information you need.'

'I'll let you know.' Hunter was suddenly in a hurry to get out of the office.

'And as far as working on the fund-raising scheme goes, I feel sure it would be possible to – eh, Arthur?'

Pine did not reply. He nodded goodbye to Hunter, and moved to the door of Rawlinson's office.

Out in the street again Hunter read a few lines of the brochure and then threw it in the gutter. The way in which Anthea had occupied her time in the past was not, after all, his affair.

Chapter Twenty

He spent the rest of the afternoon in Knightsbridge and South Kensington, checking up again on the collection plan. It is in their arrangements for collection that those who demand money with menaces fail most frequently, and although Hunter's idea was not quite foolproof, it did seem to guarantee safety for him, providing he exercised reasonable care. It was the only part of the plot that had really given him any pleasure, and he felt a rising excitement as the time approached for carrying it out.

At half-past six that evening he telephoned again, from a booth in Piccadilly. This time Moorhouse himself answered the telephone, and there was a difference in his tone. He was more abrupt, more anxious, yet at the same time somehow more guarded. Did it mean that he had informed the police, and that they were listening in?

Hunter tried to add a shade of northern accent to his voice, how successfully he could not tell.

'I'll keep it short,' he said. 'My friend rang this morning. Have you got the money?'

'Yes.'

'In one pound notes, not new, not consecutive.'

'Yes. I want to know–'

'I've got no time for answering questions. Pack the money in a zipping canvas bag. Wait for further instructions. I'll ring in the morning. Early.'

'My daughter. Anthea.' Hunter was both ashamed and ignobly pleased to hear the anxiety in Moorhouse's voice. 'Is she all right?'

'She's all right. She won't get hurt if you do as I say. Be ready for a call in the morning. Before nine o'clock.'

'But I want to know–' Hunter put down the receiver. He walked out of the booth hurriedly. There was a small glowing core of warmth in his stomach, as if he had been drinking brandy.

He breakfasted before seven-thirty next morning. The Russian exile was not up, but the young Indian smiled and bowed to him across the room. Alphonse was on duty. There was no sign of Bert. Hunter ate with a kind of spurious eagerness, but he could not taste the food in his mouth. When he had finished he asked in the reception hall for his bill. He told the Italian manageress that he was going out of London for a few days. She shrugged, to imply that it was no business of hers.

Hunter had bought a new zipping bag. He

put his things in it and deposited it in the cloakroom at Victoria station, keeping with him the old blue suitcase. He looked at his watch and saw that it was just past eight o'clock.

He took a bus to Knightsbridge, and made the last telephone call from a box outside the Underground station. This time there was no doubt about Moorhouse's anxiety. He spoke before Hunter could say anything.

'Is Anthea all right?'

Hunter pressed button A. 'Yes. Now, listen–'

'How can I be certain of that? I must know, don't you understand. I want to *know* before I pay you anything.'

'You'll have to take my word for it. She's perfectly well.'

'I want a letter from her saying so.'

Hunter experienced the irritation often felt by criminals towards victims who do not behave exactly as they should. 'If you've kept your mouth shut, and if you've got the money, she'll be all right. If we don't get the money today you can say goodbye to her.' For the moment he almost believed what he was saying. There was a sharp indrawing of breath at the other end of the telephone. 'Have you got the money ready?'

'Yes. In a canvas bag, as you said.'

'Right. Go to 191 Lower Sloane Street. It's a newsagents. Go in and ask for a letter for Mr Graham. Be there within fifteen minutes. If not, the deal's off.'

He stepped out of the box, went into the Post Office next door, and took a telegram form from the rack. Through the window he could see up and down Lower Sloane Street, and Number 191, almost opposite.

The arrangement with the newsagent was simple. A week earlier Hunter had telephoned them, using the name of William Graham, and asked if he could have letters addressed there for a fee. Yesterday a small boy, to whom he had given a shilling, had delivered a letter there. It was possible that the police might eventually trace the small boy, but by that time Hunter would be out of England. If everything went to plan, Moorhouse would come to the newsagents and collect the letter. It told him to cross the road, go into Knightsbridge tube station, and take a sixpenny ticket. He was to take a westbound train, get out at the next station, South Kensington, and enter the lift. The lift at South Kensington is unique in the Underground system. The trains travelling east and west are on different levels. At the bottom the lift picks up passengers from westbound trains. Then it moves up to a higher level and stops to pick up the eastbound ones. Finally it disgorges both at the top.

Moorhouse would get in at the bottom.

Then he was to get out at the next level and go back east as far as Piccadilly Circus station, where he was to ring up a number given in the letter. The number was fictitious, and for Moorhouse that would be the end of the trail. He was to put down the canvas bag when he entered the lift, and leave it there when he got out. Hunter would be in the lift, standing near to him. He would simply pick up the bag when he reached the top, drop it into his own larger zipping bag which would be open, and walk out.

There was a risk in the scheme. It was that a detective would be trailing Moorhouse, and would catch Hunter in the lift. But Hunter would be watching Moorhouse all the time. If he made any signal on leaving the newsagents, if there was any man at all who entered Knightsbridge station after Moorhouse, and who got into the lift with him at South Kensington and stayed in the lift, then he would not pick up the canvas bag. If the detective got out with Moorhouse on the eastbound level, and left Hunter alone in the lift, then it would be safe to collect the money. The beauty of the plan was that Moorhouse could not possibly tell the police what was in the letter containing the final instructions, and that if the detective got out on the eastbound level there was no possible way in which he could communicate with the surface in the time it took for the lift to reach the top.

If he exercised reasonable care it could not go wrong. But if it did go wrong – on his telegram form Hunter drew a pair of handcuffs.

Chapter Twenty-one

Just across the road a taxi stopped. Lord Moorhouse, a neat little bird, got out of it, paid the driver, looked questioningly at the newsagent's shop, and went in. He had a canvas bag in one hand. The taxi drove away.

A minute elapsed. Then Lord Moorhouse appeared in the door of the shop. He had opened the letter and was reading it, his lips moving. Was this some sort of signal? Hunter looked up and down Lower Sloane Street, but could see nobody moving, no recently parked car. With a decisive gesture, Lord Moorhouse thrust the letter into his pocket, looked left and right, trotted across the road and down the steps into Knightsbridge station. Quickly, but with an appearance of leisureliness, Hunter screwed up the telegram form, walked out of the Post Office and into the station. He was only a few paces behind Moorhouse.

Hunter had chosen this particular time in the morning because, although the Underground stations are busy, it is mostly with people coming out of the central London stations from their suburban homes. The number of people travelling from a station like Knightsbridge at this time is comparatively small, and in fact there were only three people behind Moorhouse at the ticket office. Hunter watched them. One, a girl wearing a neat little blue and white hat and a blue frock seemed obviously a secretary going to her office, another was an old man who limped along with a stick. But the third – the third was a man about thirty years old, with the anonymous air that is almost like the badge of a plainclothes detective. When he saw this man, Hunter felt none of the fear he had expected, but simply an increased tension throughout his body. It was as though he were encased in a rubber suit, already tightly-fitting, which had suddenly shrunk a little.

Now it was a matter of seconds in the way he timed it. Hunter waited just long enough to make sure that nobody else was entering the station, and then passed through the barrier with the ticket he had already bought. Going down in the escalator he saw Moorhouse a few steps ahead of him. He was followed by the girl, the old man and the detective – if he was a detective – in that order. They all walked down the passage to the trains. Hunter passed the old man. Moorhouse and the detective stood a few feet apart on the station platform. The train came in, and the two of them stepped into the same carriage. Hunter hesitated for a moment, then got in after them. They sat on opposite sides of the carriage and as far as he could see no communication passed between them. In any case, however, he had decided that if the detective got into the lift, and stayed in it, he would not collect the money.

They were at South Kensington station within three minutes. Hunter got out. So did Moorhouse. So did the detective. So did twenty or thirty other people. They walked along the platform again, the detective just half a dozen steps behind Moorhouse, towards a cavern that said, 'Way Out and to District Railway'. Hunter's chief feeling now was one of disgust – disgust with Moorhouse and the police for employing such an obvious plain-clothes man, disgust with Anthea for misjudging her stepfather's character, disgust with himself for working out a poor plan. Gloomily he walked along the platform, hardly bothering to keep Moorhouse and the detective in view. Gloomily turned right to the lifts, standing in the queue for them a little behind Moorhouse.

The detective was no longer there.

Hunter turned his head, caught a glimpse of the man walking down the passage towards the District Railway. He had not been a detective at all.

Moorhouse was not being followed.

Hunter felt a pulse in his throat throbbing. He was wildly excited. It's going to come off, he told himself, it's going to come off.

The lift came down. The doors opened with a clank. People poured into it. Hunter stood a little behind Moorhouse, not close to him. He looks old, Hunter thought, old and tired. He's worried about Anthea, he really does love her. Yet he could feel no sympathy in this moment, only exultation.

Now the lift stopped at the level for eastbound trains, and a mass of people came in so that the lift was completely full. For a moment Hunter felt anxiety lest Moorhouse should be unable to get out, but the little man pushed his way through.

'Goin' the wrong way, guv?' said the liftman. 'Where d'ye want to get to? Eastbound trains, this stop, not the exit.'

Moorhouse muttered something. Then he was gone. He had not been carrying the bag. Hunter did not look down, but moved forward two steps. A man in front of him said indignantly, 'There's no need to push.'

The lift gates changed, but the lift did not move. He wriggled to the side of the lift, his back to the advertisements, moved his leg cautiously, pressed against another leg, felt the pressure returned. For the life of him he dared not look down, dared not put his hand down in the direction of the bag.

The pressure against his leg was withdrawn completely, then renewed. He had been conscious only of the crowd in the lift, the bodies tightly pressed against each other which prevented him from moving along to see where Moorhouse had put the bag. Now he turned his head to see where the pressure was coming from. Standing next to him, also with her back to the advertisements, looking not at him but at a thick red neck directly ahead of her, stood the girl in the blue frock and the blue and white hat.

The lift began to move.

It took – Hunter had timed it – thirty seconds to make the journey up to the street exit. Those were the most painful seconds of his life, seconds in which an agonising battle of rival theories went on in his mind. One part of himself cursed his own stupidity in failing to take into account the possibility that the police agent might be a woman. It was not timidity, he told himself, it was merely elementary caution which dictated that he should not return the pressure, should not pick up the canvas bag, but should walk straight out of the lift, out of the station, out of the whole ridiculous plot. But there was another part of Hunter, the part that had fired a gun many years ago, and had learned in prison that men must live by calculated risks. This part of him said that women police agents do not call attention to themselves by sexual advances to suspects, that the money – more money than he could earn in years by hard work – lay almost at his feet ready to be picked up, that the risk was worth taking. And this part of him said also that there was really no room for argument, that for him there was no decision to make, the decision had been made years ago.

When the time came, when the lift stopped and the people got out and the girl in the blue dress, still without looking at him, walked with them, his action was almost automatic. He looked down, saw that the bag lay within inches of his feet, picked it up, dropped it in his own bag, zipped it up, and went out of the lift. Outside the station he saw no sign of the girl. He took a taxi to Victoria. Looking out of the taxi's small back window he could see nobody following him.

At Victoria station he went to the public lavatory and there, with the bolt firmly shot, took out Moorhouse's canvas bag, unzipped it, and turned over the brown paper parcel it contained in hands which, he was surprised to see, trembled slightly. The paper was brown and shiny, and the parcel was both tied with string and sealed with sticky tape. It seemed surprisingly small for the number of pound notes it was supposed to contain.

The string came off easily. The tape was more difficult, and by the time he had torn it open he was sweating. Inside there was more brown paper. And inside that? He found it difficult to stand up and sat down on the seat, pulling desperately at the brown paper. The whole thing was brown paper, he felt sure, it was one of those tricks often used to fool kidnappers trying to collect ransom money.

Something dropped out of the parcel on to the floor. He picked up a wad of pound notes banded together, rifled through them like a pack of cards, felt their texture, looked at their lovely greenness. Now he lifted up the parcel with utter recklessness and bundles of notes cascaded out on to the tiled lavatory floor. He made an inarticulate sound in his throat, knelt down and picked them up, felt them, and began to count the notes in each bundle. He had never thought of himself as a man particularly greedy for money, but the effect of seeing so much money, and of seeing it in this particular place, littered in bundles over the floor of this dim, secret room in which the walls were covered with scrawled obscenities, was extraordinary. This triumph for criminal Hunter over timid Hunter moved him so that for a minute or more he found it difficult not to shout or shriek. He had an impulse to unlock the door and ask everybody in the place to look at what lay on the floor.

He began to count the packets, as he pushed them methodically into his own zipping bag. He lingered over the task, and he did not realise that something was wrong until fifty packets had been counted. Then he looked at the remainder. There were a great many of them, far more than he had already packed, but surely there were not enough. Now he began to put in the rest of the packets hurriedly, throwing them in, concentrating on the counting, telling himself that he must be mistaken, and that the three hundred packets, each with a hundred pound notes in, that would make up thirty thousand pounds, positively must be here.

He had counted another thirty-five packets, making eighty-five in all, when he found the note pinned to one of the bands. It was written in a regular, almost copperplate hand that he assumed to be Moorhouse's. The note said:

I have packed up £15,000 in one pound notes as requested by you. The remaining £15,000 will be paid on my stepdaughter's return. I do this to protect her. You can be assured that I shall keep my word if you keep yours. If I do not hear from you within twelve hours of delivering this package I shall inform the police.

There was no signature. Hunter looked at the note unbelievingly, read it again, and then said aloud, 'The tricky swine. The low-down tricky swine.' He felt the indignation of a confidence trickster deceived by somebody of whose absolute integrity and innocence he has been assured.

He packed the rest of the money in the bag, tucked Moorhouse's zipper and the brown paper wrappings in as well, opened the door and walked out of the lavatory. Fifteen thousand pounds was not what they had expected and talked about, and certainly it was much less than Anthea's original seventy-five thousand – but it was still a lot of money. Since Anthea did not intend to return to her stepfather, there was no point in telephoning Moorhouse. They would get no more money. Presumably when the twelve hours had elapsed Moorhouse would carry out his threat to inform the police. This meant that they had until about nine o'clock this evening before he told them. In that time he had to make the final exchange arrangements with Westmark, book the air passages, and if possible get out of the country.

Perhaps it was a mark of some essential innocence in Hunter that it never occurred to him that Moorhouse might already have informed the police, or that he might get in touch with them before nine o'clock that evening.

Chapter Twenty-two

Yugoslavia Invites, said the travel agency poster. But they all invited, those bright unreal places where brown bodies lingered for ever by a sapphire sea, where one looked at the endless stretches of canvas in the galleries and the bits of stone stuck up in the squares which somehow one had never had the time, or even much inclination, to look at yet.

The girl behind the counter had real blonde hair, a brightly enamelled but spotty face, and very white teeth which she showed in a smile.

'Is there a flight to Belgrade?' he asked. 'Before eight o'clock tonight. I want two seats.'

She answered in tones so mellifluous that the words were almost sung. 'No flights to Belgrade today, I'm afraid. The Belgrade service operates only three days a week.'

'Or anywhere else in Yugoslavia.'

'There are no flights available elsewhere in Yugoslavia for the whole of this month,' she sang triumphantly.

'What about Italy?'

'There are flights to Rome, Milan, Naples.' He was about to say eagerly that any of them would do when his precipitancy was checked. 'I can get you on a flight to Naples – let me see – next Thursday. The others would take rather longer.'

He dug his nails into the palms of his hands. This conversation, with its picture of a man who wanted to get out of England in a hurry, was becoming altogether too memorable in case of future questioning.

'It's like this,' he said, appealing a little desperately to the spotty enamelled goddess on the other side of the counter. 'We've just got an unexpected holiday, this friend of mine and I, it starts today and we don't want to waste any time, only got a couple of weeks you know. We want to go somewhere hot. And we want to go today, or perhaps by a night flight if there's nothing earlier.'

She nodded like a blonde mandarin. Then she went away and talked to a man inside a glass cubicle. The man came out. Hunter had to control a growing feeling of panic.

'I'm afraid we can't offer you anything at all today, sir. Not for Europe.'

'I see. Oh, well–' He was anxious now only to get away.

'The only thing we have is two cancellations on the midnight flight to Tangier.'

'Why, that would be splendid.' Feeling that he had betrayed too much enthusiasm he added, 'It isn't just what I wanted, but we can get across to Gib., and then go to Torremolinos perhaps. I've always wanted to see Malaga.' His voice tailed off. They were paying him no attention. With a nod and a smile the man had gone back inside his cubicle. The girl was writing out details of the tickets.

'Return?' she asked.

'Single. We shall come back by train, I think.'

She flashed her smile at him. 'If you're coming back from Spain, don't forget to make your train reservations in advance. You can't board any of the fast trains otherwise.'

Chapter Twenty-three

The Chinese girl showed him in again to the great room overlooking the park. This time she wore a black frock with an emerald dragon on it, buttoned tight to the neck. Her arms were bare, and on both of them there were large bruises. In her eyes, as she opened the door and for a moment looked at him, Hunter seemed to see some message that he could not understand. Then she looked down at the floor, and the momentary impression was gone.

This time Westmark's silk shirt was peach-coloured, his cuff-links large pearls. The 1803 Madeira was produced and appreciated. He talked about the weather, about going to Ascot, about a yacht he thought of buying which had been offered him by a member of a certain Royal family, a family that must be nameless.

'You will know who it is I mean, I expect. It is a nice yacht and I should like to help him, but that is not easy.' His gentle smile expressed his sorrow that it was impossible to help everybody.

Hunter became impatient. He opened the zipping bag, took out the packets of money, and put them on an inlaid rosewood table. Westmark stopped talking. His fingers stroked the stem of the Madeira glass.

'How much money is there?'

'Fifteen thousand. In ones.'

'We were speaking of more than that.'

'That was talk. This is money.' Hunter spoke with a confidence he did not quite feel.

'Where do you want to change it?'

'In Tangier.'

The German nodded. 'Is the money hot?'

'No.'

'Where did it come from? If it is your own, why not write me a cheque?' Hunter had no answer. He had not expected such questions. Westmark sipped his Madeira. 'People do not often come to me with a sum of money like this, and in pound notes too. They write a cheque. I make a piece of property, or something of equal value, available to them in Gibraltar or Valencia or Naples. I have agents in all these places. I have an agent in Tangier, naturally. Or a bank account is opened–'

'You told me all that before. And I told you I wanted your agent to give me cash. Cash is what you've got there on the table.'

'Where did the money come from, Mr Hunter?' Hunter jerked back his head in alarm. 'Yes, I know your name. Your face was familiar to me, but at the time I could not place it. I have done so since.'

'Well?'

Westmark shrugged. There was something epicene about him, in spite of his size. 'I have to know the names of those I deal with. It was foolish to call yourself Smith. I know what has happened to you. Where would you get fifteen thousand pounds?'

'It came from a bank. And I didn't steal it. Somebody gave it to me.'

'Very well. I am sorry. We cannot do business.'

I mustn't let him see what this means to me, Hunter thought. He sat on his striped chair, sipped the Madeira, and said nothing.

'If you acknowledged that the money was hot, that you had obtained it in some way that you wished to keep to yourself, then we might have arranged something. I have my own terms for hot money.'

'It's not hot. I told you that. They're all ones, and they're not new. They're not in sequence. They can't be checked.'

Westmark went on as if he had not spoken. 'But you insist that it came from a bank, that somebody gave it to you. Very well. Go and pay it into your own bank, and give me a cheque. Or go and give it to somebody else. I want nothing to do with it.'

He's got me by the short hairs, Hunter thought, and he knows it. Bitterly he said, 'All right. The money's hot, though not in the way you mean. It can't be traced. But I want to go abroad, and I can't take it with me. What's the deal?'

Westmark drank the rest of his Madeira at a gulp. His eyes watched Hunter. 'Why is it important that you leave England in such a hurry?'

'That's nothing to do with it. Or with you.'

'Very well. Fifty per cent.'

'So that's how the good life's paid for.' Hunter began to throw the packets of money back into the bag. Westmark watched him throw a few back, and then spoke again.

'Come now, Mr Hunter. Be reasonable.

There is a risk connected with this money, or you would not want to get rid of it so quickly. I take the risk, not you. All you have to do is to go to my agent in Tangier, Mr Kadiska, and he will make available to you seven thousand five hundred pounds in any currency you care to name.'

'If you honour the agreement.'

'As I said to you before, you will not find anybody to tell you that Theo Westmark does not honour his agreements. If I wished to cheat you I should agree to any terms you wished. But I have said already, take away the money if that is what you want. I shall forget that you have ever been here.'

There was no time to get in touch with Dawes and make fresh arrangements. But Hunter went on putting money into the bag. Suddenly Westmark laughed, a rich musical sound.

'You are not an easy man to deal with, Mr Hunter. Do you suppose I have built up my business as – what shall I call it? – an honest broker – by cheating my clients? I told you before that there must be mutual trust in our affairs. I trust you, when you say that my agents will not be arrested when they try to pass this money. You do assure me of that, don't you?'

'I've told you, there's nothing wrong with the money.'

'I accept your assurance,' Westmark said

gravely. 'And now, if you wish, I will give you a cheque. You can walk out and post it to Tangier to await your arrival. It will mean nothing, but if it soothes your feeling of anxiety...'

'No. Write to Kadiska, your agent, as you suggested. That's good enough. But let's talk about the terms.'

Westmark held the glass up to the light. 'Sweet, rich, strong. It is nectar. I am afraid that you do not appreciate it.'

The cloying smell was in his nostrils again. He said again, doggedly, 'Let's talk about the terms.'

'But what is there to talk about?'

'You said fifty per cent. I'll pay ten. That gives you fifteen hundred pounds for writing a letter.'

Westmark shook his head. 'It is not for writing a letter, but for taking a risk with something I know nothing about. I could not do it for less than forty per cent. It would be foolish.'

In the end they settled for twenty-five per cent. Instead of having twenty-eight thousand five hundred pounds for conversion in Tangier, he and Anthea would have twelve thousand two hundred and fifty.

'Another glass of wine?'

'No, thank you.'

Like a great cat Westmark walked over to the table, and stood looking at the money.

He did not touch it. 'Then let me wish you all the luck in the world.'

He left the room. Westmark was still looking at the money on the table. The Chinese girl appeared, eyes downcast, and went with him to the door. There she said something.

'What's that?' Hunter asked. 'What did you say?'

'Your name is Hunter.'

'Yes.'

'It is not good for you to come here. There is a man–'

The door of Westmark's room opened, and his bulk filled the doorway. His voice was soft. 'Kitten, are you talking to Mr Hunter? You know I do not like you to talk to my guests. Come here.'

The girl almost ran to him. The cosmetic mask did not change, but Hunter sensed the terror behind it. He let himself out.

Chapter Twenty-four

He was the only person to get off the train at Blanting, and he left the padlocked zipping bag with the money in it, in the luggage office at the station. As he left the village behind, and turned off into a field of wheat, following the route he had taken with Anthea, the sky darkened. Presently it began to rain, no more than a few drops at first, but then with thick persistence. Hunter was wearing a dark suit and thin town shoes. As he walked along, skirting the edge of fields, walking over tracks already used by cattle, he trod in mud that squelched persistently underfoot and that once or twice oozed thinly over the edge of his shoe.

After half an hour's walking he began to feel unsure that he was going in the right direction. How stupid he had been not to ask Anthea to draw a map, he reflected. He felt mingled relief and alarm when he turned into yet another field and came almost face to face with a farm labourer trudging along in sou'wester hat and black oilskin cape.

The man was smoking a pipe. He took it out of his mouth to say, 'Arternoon.'

'Good afternoon.' Hunter tried to move into the shelter of a small bush which immediately pelted him with raindrops.

'It's a wet 'un.'

'It is indeed.' He spoke with what he felt to be odiously false joviality. 'I seem to have lost my way a bit. I've come from Blanting.'

'Might help if you said where you were tryin' to get to.'

'Of course. It's the nearest village – over in this direction, I think.' He pointed wildly.

The man shook his head. 'Not that way. Bassington estate that way, old Manor

House. Nearest village's Leddenham, couple of mile across the fields, straight as you can go. Then you come to the road, turn right and matter of a quarter of a mile along go sharp left–'

He ceased to listen, waited until the man had finished giving directions which were both long and elaborate, and then offered thanks. The labourer looked at him curiously. 'You're welcome. Didn't come out prepared for weather, eh?' Hunter laughed feebly. 'If you're stayin' in Leddenham best place is the Black Bull.' He stuck his pipe in his mouth again, nodded goodbye, and was gone.

There's a man who won't forget me, Hunter thought. But at least he knew in which direction the estate lay. He plunged on through thick grass, nettles, brambles, until he reached the barbed wire. The wood was on his right – he had gone a hundred yards too far, that was all.

As he reached the edge of the wood, the rain stopped. He wiped his face and hair with a handkerchief, but water continued to trickle down his neck and to drop from his suit. There was water in his shoes, too, as he trod on bracken up a barely marked path. Suddenly he was in the glade, and looking round he saw that he had come along the overgrown path he had seen leading on through the wood, when they had come here before together.

'Anthea,' he called, and called again. His voice sounded strange in the unstirring wood, strange and – although he did not think of himself as an imaginative man – frightening. There was no answer, but perhaps sound did not carry far in such surroundings. He wiped his head and face again. He was shivering a little, possibly with the beginnings of a cold.

Slowly, reluctantly, he began to push a way through the brambles that, as they had done before, sprang back at him. He had only a few yards to go, yet he was shivering uncontrollably by the time he had pushed a way through to where the stone hut stood, and there was unmistakable terror in his voice as he cried her name again.

She did not answer. He did not know what it was he feared, what sort of ultimate betrayal he expected to find inside the hut. She had left the place, changed her mind suddenly about the whole plot – that would be like her. Or it had all been some sort of trick played on him – that possibility had, as he knew, always been present somewhere in his mind. Or she had told somebody about the den in spite of her promise not to do so, some secret enemy, and she lay within the hut, dead.

He did not want to prove his fears, or to know the details of her betrayal if she had betrayed him. He did not want to open the hut door. But had he not already realised that he had reached a point from which there was no turning back? He walked to the door of the hut, and pushed. The door creaked and opened.

The hut was empty. The dust lay on the floor, as it had done before. Anthea had never come here, nobody had come here. Had he not accepted this as a possibility? Yet now that he was confronted with the act of betrayal, now that the hut offered its silent evidence that she had cynically rejected all that they had talked about, he could not believe it. He stumbled to the door again and out of it, walked round the hut looking for footprints (but there were no footprints except his own), leant against the side of the hut staring at the green bushes in front of him, and mouthing unintelligible words. There was nothing to be seen here, and nothing to be done. When he looked round the scene that should have been the victorious climax of their planning, tears came to his eyes and ran down unchecked.

As he left the hut and stumbled away, pushing through again to the glade, thin sunlight filtered through the poplars. The tears were still in his eyes, but as he walked back, stepping recklessly in puddles, smearing his shoes with mud and filling them with water, he sought for an answer to the question; why had she done it? What purpose could there be in a plot which left him with fifteen thousand pounds in ransom money, to use as he wished?

Was there, then, another sort of explanation, one which did not involve betrayal? Had her stepfather discovered what she meant to do, locked her up, and handed over the money in order to have him arrested afterwards while in possession of it? Had Roger Sennett somehow discovered the plot, and told Lord Moorhouse? When he got out of the wood the day was bright and warm. On the dripping branches, in the sunlight, birds sang. He had recovered his faith in Anthea, and he knew what he meant to do.

Chapter Twenty-five

The headlines met him as he got off the train at Waterloo, just before five o'clock. *Peer's Daughter Kidnapped*, he read, and *Society Beauty Held to Ransom*. Moorhouse had not kept his word, then – he had realised, perhaps, that any kidnapper who meant to claim the further fifteen thousand pounds would have been in touch with him again at once. Or was this, in some way impossible for him to understand, part of Moorhouse's own plan? He bought the papers, and read the stories. They described Anthea variously as 'a beautiful society debutante,' as 'a girl who shunned the bright lights to help her stepfather, Lord Moorhouse, in his work for Colonial development,' and as 'one of London's slum-going smart set, engaged to the Honourable Roger Sennett, son of Lord Broughleigh.' Nothing was said about the fifteen thousand pounds that Moorhouse had paid over, but there was an interview with him in which he said that his daughter was fond of practical jokes, and that he still hoped she might be playing some sort of joke now. The interview went on:

'If you discovered that this was some sort of practical joke now, would you be very angry?' I asked.

'Not at all. I am too anxious about Anthea's safety. I want her to come home.'

'If the practical joke theory were right, the men who rang up would be friends of hers, and in the joke as well.'

'That's right.'

'Did they sound as if they were joking?'

Lord Moorhouse's mouth set in a grim, hard line. 'They did not. They sounded as if they were the scum of the earth.'

The case was the first of its kind in England, and the evening papers played it up accordingly. There were several photographs of

Anthea, in riding kit, stroking a dog, in evening dress, with the caption HAVE YOU SEEN HER? There was an interview with an unnamed police inspector in charge of the case, who expressed confidence that Miss Moorhouse would be found within the next forty-eight hours.

Reading these stories, he felt his idea that Moorhouse was somehow keeping Anthea prisoner rather shaken. Supposing, then, that somebody else was responsible for her disappearance, what was the likely course of events? Bert from the Cosmos would undoubtedly go to the police and tell his story, but there was nothing in it positively incriminating to Hunter. Why should a man who had had Anthea as a mistress try to kidnap her? It was possible that the police might keep a watch on places of exit from the country. Did it matter? He shrugged away the thought. The plane for Tangier did not leave till midnight, and he did not want to be on it without Anthea.

Chapter Twenty-six

Within the flat there were voices. He stood a moment on the landing, strangely reluctant to use the key. Then he turned it in the lock, opened the door, hesitated again in the hall, put down the blue suitcase and the zipping bag, and opened the living room door.

'Why, *Bill!*' Anna swung her legs off the sofa, pushed away her woman's magazine, got up. 'We were talking about you. You're wet, Bill, you're awfully wet.'

'Talk of the devil,' Charlie Cash said. He was sunk in the big shabby armchair with the webbing gone at the bottom, and there was a bottle of beer by his side. 'I was asking Anna where I could find you. She said she didn't know.'

'And in you come like the Prince in the fairy tale.'

'Or the wicked uncle.'

They were glad to see him, there was no doubt about it. They enveloped him in a blanket of affection which was quite unlike anything he had known in his relationship with Anthea, a relationship all ice and fire. He knew the warmth and the protective quality of the blanket well enough, but the time had gone by when he could roll up in it and think himself happy. So now he looked from one to the other of them, and answered the question that Anna had not asked.

'I'd like a bath and a change of clothes. I should like that very much.'

'And shoes,' she cried, refusing to see any implication of speedy departure in what he had just said. 'They're simply filthy. All over mud. You might have been walking through fields in them. Charlie, go and talk to Bill in the bath while I get him some clean clothes.' Now she came up to him and kissed him on the cheek.

Five minutes later he was in the bath with a glass of whisky in his hand, and Charlie was sitting on the bathroom stool drinking beer.

'What I wanted to say was this, that you went off half-cock when you left here.'

His body was exposed to the water, he seemed to feel it seeping through the flesh, warming the chilled bones. He drained half the glass of whisky and felt corresponding warmth in his stomach. Where was the liquid that would warm the heart? 'I don't understand you.'

Charlie, unusually, was embarrassed. 'About you and Anna, I got no call to interfere. I know that. You want to leave her, I think you're a fool, but it's not my business.

I'm talking about a job, about you being finished in TV. You're wrong about that.'

He went on to explain. There was this TV research firm, Bill knew the kind of thing, audience research, what markets were best for what products, why C and D groups switched off at certain times of the day no matter what programme was on, what programmes got real audience participation, that kind of thing. 'They're looking for an assistant general manager, and it could be you, Bill.'

Clouds of steam came up from him. 'You mean you mentioned my name and they didn't flinch?'

'Hell, no, why should they flinch about something that happened way back in the dark ages? We all killed people in the war and crowed about it. You're out as a TV personality, agreed, but for the rest of it you're carrying a chip on your shoulder.'

The bathroom door opened. Anna put her head round it. 'There's a man on the telephone. His name's Westmark. Shall I tell him you're here?'

'Westmark.' He sat up, moved to get out of the bath, thought again. 'Say you may be in touch with me. If so, you'll ask me to telephone. Try to find out what he wants.'

Her head disappeared. 'I thought you just wanted his name for an article you were writing,' Charlie said.

'That's what I said.'

'Westmark's dangerous.'

'You said he was reliable.'

'So he is. But dangerous if you try to play any tricks with him. What have you...' Charlie shut his thin mouth at the sight of Hunter's expression. 'Not my business, all right, I know. But how about the other thing, Bill? How about coming along with me to see these people?'

The heat, the real passionate heat, was going out of the water. 'Give me the towel, Charlie.'

'What about it?'

'No use. It's too late.'

'Too late,' Charlie echoed indignantly. 'That's nonsense, Bill. Too late for what? It's never too late.'

He wrapped himself in the big towel, the warm protective thing, but inside him there remained an area of cold. 'It's been too late for a long time, Charlie, too late for me. I told you before. When something like this happens you have to make a clean break. It's the only way.'

'You never do it,' Charlie said. 'You keep on coming back. That's why you're here. Don't you want to know what I found out about that girl who calls herself a model?'

'Tanya Broderick? Not particularly. Does it matter?'

'She's never been inside, but she's no

more of a genuine model than I am. She plays around with people on the edge of crime – not the real big boys but the hangers-on, understrappers you might call 'em.' Charlie said slowly, 'There are three or four men she's mixed up with now – she never has just one boyfriend at a time. One of them is Brannigan, Paddy Brannigan. Didn't you say you knew him?'

The mirror had steamed over. He rubbed away reflectively and saw himself, a red-haired ogre in a bath towel.

'Didn't you?'

'It was a long time ago, Charlie,' he said. 'Too long.'

In the bedroom Anna had put out a good grey tweed suit, clean handkerchief, shirt, socks, shoes. It was all part of the warmth he understood, but could not feel, that a fly-button was missing from the trousers and that there was a hole in the toe of one sock. Before putting on the suit he looked in the second drawer of the chest of drawers, the one that almost always stuck. This time it opened smoothly. The gun lay beneath spare sheets, black, shiny, surprisingly small. He broke it to see that it was loaded, dressed, and put it into his hip pocket.

Back in the living room Anna stared at him mournfully. 'You're going away again.'

'Yes. What's Westmark's number?'

'On the pad by the telephone.'

Charlie got up, drained his beer. 'I'm off. Ta very much for the beer, sweetie. Be seeing you. Goodbye, Bill.' He kissed Anna lightly on the forehead. As he went out he did not look at Hunter.

Now that they were alone, Anna compassionately stared at him. 'Are you going to ring up that man?'

'Later, perhaps. Not now.'

'You're in trouble.'

'You might say so.'

'Charlie says Westmark's a currency fiddler, does it in a big way. Says he's a bad man to get mixed up with.'

'Charlie should know. He gave me Westmark's name.'

'Are you leaving the country?'

'I was. Now it looks a bit doubtful.'

She wandered over to the mantelpiece, took a sweet from the box there, bit it. 'There's someone else. You're taking her with you.'

'There's nobody else, Anna. Not at present, anyway. I'm just going out to play a game. Find the lady, you might call it.' He touched her shoulder. It was firm and warm. 'You've always been good to me. Better than I deserve.' Why is it always the stale, sentimental words one uses, he wondered?

The usual easy tears were in her eyes. 'You're in some sort of trouble. I don't know what it is, but I can tell it's bad trouble.

Don't do anything silly.'

'I've done such a lot of silly things in my life that one or two more don't matter.'

She put her hand on his arm, timidly. 'You think too much about the past. Really it doesn't matter all that much.'

'It does to me. Sometimes I think that the past is the only thing that's real.' He broke away from her, muttering something – he could not have said exactly what – and left the flat.

Chapter Twenty-seven

To place one's head deliberately in the lion's mouth – is that the best way of making sure that one is not eaten? Would Moorhouse recognise him as one of the people in the lift? People had swarmed into it from the eastbound train, and it was impossible for Moorhouse to remember them all. Moreover, Hunter had stayed behind him on the escalator and had stood behind him in the lift. But fear of recognition, in any case, was comparatively unimportant to him now. To find Anthea, or to find out why she had not come to the den – did anything else matter? Boldly he walked up the steps of the house in Cavendish Square, and rang the bell.

The door was opened by a butler – could it, in these days, be a butler? Some sort of grave deferential flunkey, at least, with the jowly dignity that is so rarely found among genuine aristocrats.

'Lord Moorhouse,' Hunter said. 'It's in connection with his stepdaughter's disappearance.'

The jowly dignity was undisturbed. Hunter was asked into a hall like the scene from a film set. A subdued light from a chandelier illuminated, more or less, pieces of heavy mahogany furniture and huge armchairs, stretching away into the middle distance. Brownish paintings stared down from the walls. He walked across to one of them and read the gold plaque beneath. 'Edward John Moorhouse, 1818-1884. Master Mariner.' The name signed to the painting was that of a living Academician. Why, it's a fake, Hunter thought. The old devil's got some hack to paint his ancestors from old photographs. He was moving on to the next painting when a cough came from behind him.

'Lord Moorhouse will see you now, sir. If you will come this way.'

He followed a broad back through one great room and another, and then along a corridor littered with vases and bits of statuary. This is the treatment, he told himself, the old English home treatment they put on for the benefit of ex-IRA barbarians who come to pay a visit. Like the family portraits, it's a fake. He was not altogether satisfied with this reassurance. Even if this was just the treatment for barbarians, he had to admit that it was impressive. He tried to imagine Anthea in these surroundings, and failed. Surely she must have rebelled against them? And so she had, he reminded himself. What was the kidnap plot but an act of rebellion?

The room into which he was ushered at last was comparatively small, almost cosy. Standard sets of standard authors lined two walls, there was a recording machine and two desks, a large one at which Lord Moorhouse now sat, and a smaller one with a typewriter on it. This was the study, then? A man stood with his back to Moorhouse, looking out of the window. He did not turn round.

'I understand you have some information about my stepdaughter, Mr–'

'Hunter.' Moorhouse looked clean still and birdlike, but the weariness Hunter had noticed in the lift was now more marked. The bird's eye was not so bright and quick, an edge of sharpness had gone, he was more obviously an old man. He gave no sign of recognising Hunter. 'I'm a friend of hers,' he went on. 'I saw her on Saturday night. I thought it might be useful to you to know that – I don't know when she disappeared–'

'On Monday morning.' Moorhouse sounded tired, not very interested. 'She was at home on Sunday. It's kind of you, Mr Hunter, but I don't think Saturday night will help very much. What we're really looking for is somebody who saw her on Monday. She rang up a friend early on Monday morning, and made an arrangement to go shopping.'

'I see.' Anthea had kept to the arrangement so far, then. Discouragement was visible in every line of Moorhouse's face, every word he spoke. The idea that he could have had anything to do with Anthea's disappearance was obviously wrong. Hunter was about to say that he supposed he could not be of any help, when the man at the window turned round and revealed the bright smile and the eager doggish salesman's look of Inspector Crambo.

'Mr Hunter? We meet again. It's a small world, as they say.'

'Inspector Crambo is handling the – the investigation,' Moorhouse said wearily. 'You know Mr Hunter, Inspector?'

'I've had the pleasure of meeting him before, yes.'

'I didn't see in the papers that you were in charge,' Hunter said, before he could stop himself.

'Or you wouldn't have come along here, eh?' Crambo's meaningless laugh somehow made his words more offensive. 'Keep out of the way of the police, as my old mum always used to say, only mix with nice people. Right she was, too. But this is a funny sort of coincidence, now, wouldn't you agree to that? Except, no doubt, that you could improve my phrasing.'

'I don't know what you mean.'

Crambo did not speak for a moment. He was looking at Hunter, not at his face but somewhere about halfway down his body. Could there be some mark on his clothes, Hunter wondered, and did not dare look down. Now Crambo spoke, but almost absent-mindedly, as though he were talking to fill in time while he worked out some difficult problem in mental arithmetic.

'First of all you turn up in this affair of Melville Bond. You seem to have quite a bit of knowledge about Bond being mixed up with Mr Nicholas Mekles.'

'I've already told you, I simply used the information I was given by my research assistant.'

'I know you explained, but it was a bit of a coincidence you must agree. I mean, you just happened to ask Mr Mekles about this chap Bond, and it just happened that he'd committed suicide a few hours earlier. That's right, isn't it?'

'Are you certain it was suicide?'

'That was the verdict at the inquest. There was a witness, remember.'

Hunter was stung into useless speech. 'Did you know that the witness was a woman who had occupied the flat she was in for only three weeks, an associate of criminals?' Crambo was no longer looking at Hunter, and seemed to have worked out his problem. At least he had regained his normal brisk salesman's manner. It was almost with amusement that he said, 'Yes. We knew that, Mr Hunter.'

'Did you notice the two long scratches under the window that might have been made by a man's heels as he was forced back out of it?'

'Or his toes as he scrambled out awkwardly. Bond had a leg injury in the war, did you know that? It would have been quite a job for him to climb out on to that sill.'

Hunter was disconcerted. 'But you never questioned the girl's story.'

'Didn't we? How do you know?'

'Why...'

'Miss Broderick was under questioning for several hours. She's a cool customer – as cool as a cucumber if you'll forgive the cliché.'

Moorhouse had been listening impatiently. Now he interrupted. 'Inspector, what is all this? Has it really any connection with my daughter's disappearance?'

Crambo scratched his head in mock perplexity. 'I just don't know, sir. They say at the Yard that Crambo walks all round the garden looking at the flowers, but in the end he gets to the compost heap.'

'What does that mean?'

'It means that, unless I'm much mistaken, something here stinks. This man Hunter is a convicted criminal. He had a job on television which he gave up after an altercation with the financier Nicholas Mekles–'

'Mekles. Oh, yes. I've heard of him.' Whatever Lord Moorhouse had heard about Nicholas Mekles was plainly nothing good.

'I expect you have. An altercation about a man named Bond, who had just committed suicide. As you've heard, he seems to doubt that it was suicide. Now he comes in here, saying he's a friend of your daughter. He said he had some information to give, but he seemed to be looking for it, not giving it. Do you see what I mean when I talk about the compost heap?' Turning to Hunter, Crambo asked, 'How long have you known Miss Moorhouse?'

'For some weeks.'

'After you left your television job?'

'I met her a few days afterwards, yes.'

'And you saw her on Saturday night?'

'Yes.'

'You're living in London?'

'That's right.'

'You saw her in London, then?'

'Of course.'

'Ah, you're one of those "of course" chaps. Always been too slow myself, too coarse to be of course, if you see what I mean.' He covered his mouth with his hand, like a man trying to conceal a belch. 'What did you talk about at this meeting on Saturday night now? Did she say anything important, interesting, anything that indicated why she might have disappeared? Sinister men following her, you know, anything like that?'

With the feeling that he was falling into some obvious trap, Hunter said slowly, 'She mentioned something about a man following her. A tall man with a slight limp.'

'Aha. Any further details?'

'She thought he'd been watching the house – this house, I mean.'

Crambo wagged an admonitory finger at Lord Moorhouse, sunk in gloom at his desk. There was something almost indecent about his levity. 'That confirms what Mr Sennett told us. The mysterious stranger. The man with the limp. Very nice touch, that limp. Anything more about him, now? Bowler hat, sports car round the corner, turned his foot inwards with a special sort of twist, anything like that?'

There was something ominous, surely, about this levity. 'I think she said he was bareheaded. There was nothing else. You must remember that it was a casual remark, nothing more than that.'

'Of course.' Crambo looked pleased. 'There you are. Managed one myself. You didn't see this man, I suppose, Mr Hunter?'

'No.'

'And she didn't point him out to you at this place you met, wherever it was. Where was it, by the way? In London, yes, I know that. Of course. But where would it have been?'

'It was in a hotel.'

'In your hotel, would it have been? In the Cosmos in Pimlico? That's where you usually met, I believe.'

The moment had an impact as appalling as that in which one breaks a glass. Hunter looked round for a chair, saw a leathery club armchair across the room, made his way to it on rubbery legs, sat down. This removed him from the vicinity of Crambo, and the inspector also moved, strolling across from the window to the typist's desk a foot or two from the armchair. He perched on this desk, hitching up his trousers to reveal finely-polished, rather pointed black shoes, and elegant striped socks. Only Moorhouse stayed unmoving at the big desk, with head hunched into his shoulders.

'You've been talking to Bert,' Hunter said.

'Bert?' The inspector raised an eyebrow. 'Oh, yes. Robert Manton, waiter. Came forward very promptly to give information, public spirited citizen and all that. Didn't seem to like you much, said you threatened him.'

'He didn't tell you that he had tried to blackmail me.'

'Is that so?' Crambo was odiously polite. 'Now, what would he be able to blackmail you about?'

'Miss Moorhouse...' He stopped, out of pity for the old man at the desk. But why should he feel pity? He remembered the look on Anthea's face as she bit her fingernail and told him that her stepfather had made a pass at her. It occurred to him for the first time that the story might not be true.

'You were very friendly with her? She visited you at the hotel. She was your mistress?'

Hunter was saved from the need for an immediate reply, by the old man's gesture of protest. Moving a little in his chair he spoke. 'Anthea was always a wild girl, Inspector, but nothing more, I assure you of that. Her mother died when she was a child, you know. She never settled down, somehow, I don't know how it was, she has never settled down to any interest. There's the PFC, of course, I was glad she interested herself in that. If she was friendly with this young man, I am sure it was an innocent relationship.'

'I'm sorry.' Crambo did not look in the least sorry. 'Your daughter visited this man's room, day after day, and stayed there for hours at a time, according to the hotel waiter.'

'But must you – these details are objectionable. Are they important?'

'They are. Miss Moorhouse has disappeared. You think it may be a practical joke of hers. I doubt it. Now here is a man with a record of violence, and not much money. He knew her well. It's important to know how well. What do you say, Mr Hunter? Was she your mistress?'

'Yes.'

'The waiter recognised her and tried to blackmail you?'

'Yes. He saw an old *Tatler* with her photograph in it.'

'That was why you moved out of the Cosmos so suddenly.'

'Yes.' At least, he realised, the attempt at blackmail gave a reasonable explanation for his departure from the hotel.

'You say that Saturday was the last time you saw Miss Moorhouse. You left the Cosmos on Tuesday. Weren't you surprised that she hadn't got in touch with you?'

'A little. But it wasn't all that unusual.'

'Have you tried to get in touch with her?'

'No. She doesn't much like me doing that. Telephoning her at home here, I mean.' It was a good thing probably to stick to the truth as nearly as he could. 'I thought she might be away. Then I saw the paper.'

Crambo got off the table, walked six steps up and down the room, wheeled round and said sharply, 'What did you come here for?'

'I've told you. To help–'

'You saw her on Saturday, she disappeared on Monday. What help did you think that could be?' Crambo spoke almost contemptuously. 'We know something about Miss Moorhouse's movements on Monday. I don't know whether it will be news to you or not. She rang up this friend, Mary Winter, and arranged to go shopping. She never arrived at Miss Winter's flat. She did, however, go to the offices of the Patriotic Fellowship Circle. She arrived there at about ten-thirty, discussed with the colonial secretary, Mr Pine, arrangements about some canvassing they were to do that evening, and left about a quarter of an hour later. That's the last information we have about her.'

For a moment Moorhouse was roused from his abstraction. 'That was the one thing,' he said, 'the one thing that interested her. I blame myself – perhaps I didn't encourage her sufficiently.' His voice died away.

It was a piece of typical over-elaboration on Anthea's part to deviate from their original plan by calling on the PFC and making arrangements for future canvassing. But why had Crambo said nothing about the money.

'I love Anthea,' he said. 'I want to find out what has happened to her. That's why I came here.'

There was a long moment in which Crambo's curious, light-coloured eyes stared into Hunter's. Then the detective laughed, an easy, vulgar laugh that destroyed the tension between them. 'Do you know, I'm beginning to put on the pressure like a real American detective. The AC said to me the other day, "Crambo," he said, "You've been reading too many of these American thrillers. You're beginning to talk out of the corner of your mouth. Watch it, Crambo," he said, "or you'll never get promotion." Quite right, too, but you know what it is. Sometimes your feelings run away with you.'

To this illusionist's patter he made no reply, suspecting it to be a cover for some question meant to disconcert him. But no question came. Humming a little, Crambo turned his back, went to the window again.

'You mean there's nothing else you want to ask?'

The detective turned round. He was smiling. 'Not another thing. You might let me know where I can get in touch with you. Don't want to lose contact, you know.'

He gave the address and telephone number of Anna's flat. 'Is that all? I'm free to go now.' Somehow, he could not believe it.

Crambo responded with his odiously self-satisfied, falsely friendly smile. 'Of course.'

Hunter said goodbye to Moorhouse, who did not answer. Walking out of the house, hurrying away across the Square, he felt as if he had been released again from prison.

Chapter Twenty-eight

The flat was in Hallam Street, on the second floor. He put his finger on the bell, and kept it there until Roger Sennett opened the door. His dark face looked not only sullen, but angry. 'Yes?'

'My name is Hunter. I want to talk to you.'

The young man looked at him. 'If you're selling something, I don't want to buy it.'

'It's about Anthea, Anthea Moorhouse.'

Sennett stared at him from dark deep-set eyes. 'All right. Come in.'

Books and papers were scattered about the living room. Hunter looked round for some sign of Anthea here, a hairslide or a handkerchief, but saw none.

Sennett said abruptly, 'I'm going out to dinner in a quarter of an hour, so it'll have to be quick. Have we met before? I seem to know your face.'

'I was in a Pimlico club that was raided

one night. I helped Anthea – Miss Moorhouse – get away.'

'You were the good Samaritan.' Sennett laughed. His manner had thawed a little. 'Have a drink.'

Sipping his sherry, Hunter said, 'You know she has disappeared – been kidnapped?'

'I read the papers, yes.'

'You don't seem to be very upset.'

Sennett peered at him as though he were trying to find the answer to a puzzle. 'Should I be?'

'You were more or less engaged, isn't that so?'

'Did she tell you that?' Sennett pushed aside newspapers and put down his sherry glass on a table. 'I haven't heard anything yet to convince me that you have any right to ask questions.'

The doorbell rang. Sennett got up to answer it. Hunter had a sudden feeling that Anthea had rung the bell, a conviction so strong that it was difficult to restrain himself from going to the door of the room in which he sat. When Sennett came back, however, he was accompanied by a tall young girl with a good figure, whose blonde hair was pulled back in a pony tail.

'Rosemary, this is Mr Hunter, who's come to ask some questions about Anthea. He seems to think I'm engaged to her.' The girl laughed lightly, a pleasant sound. Sennett peered again. There was a kind of lowering distinction in his face. 'Rosemary Felton and I got ourselves engaged last week.'

'I know you,' the girl said suddenly. 'You're that TV man who resigned because of some old scandal. It was a dirty trick they played on you, I thought, digging up all that old stuff.'

'Thank you. And congratulations.' Hunter looked from one to the other of them. He did not doubt what Sennett had said, and was puzzled. 'But I understood – after all, you came to the dance hall with Anthea.'

'Let's get this straight, though I still don't know what business it is of yours.' Sennett sounded a little exasperated, but not at all embarrassed. 'I've known Anthea since she was a kid. She lived only a few miles away from our place in Hampshire. Did she tell you that?'

'No.'

'Well, it's so. Her stepfather's been pretty keen that I should look after her, keep her out of trouble, that sort of thing. I tagged along to the dance hall to keep her out of trouble, though in the end I got into some myself. Her stepfather – Lord Moorhouse – was keen that we should get married. Was that what Anthea told you?'

'I suppose so,' he said uncertainly. What exactly had Anthea told him? Nothing, it was true, that exactly contradicted what Sennett was saying, yet somehow what she said had possessed a different meaning. 'But you were never engaged?'

'Or near to it. Now, Mr Hunter, I'm taking a girl I *am* engaged to out to dinner. The door's behind you.'

'Roger, you're so *rude,*' Rosemary Felton said. 'Five minutes don't matter that much. Can't you see Mr Hunter is worried?'

The young man turned to her quite furiously. 'And why the hell should I care if he is worried. I don't know who he is, and I don't want to know. What right has he got to come in here asking me a lot of questions about my relations with Anthea? If you hadn't been here I'd have thrown him out on his neck.'

The girl was two inches taller than Sennett. She looked at him adoringly, and said to Hunter, 'It might help if you explained. You do see that.'

Hunter looked at their faces, Sennett's dark and flushed, the face of a Victorian Colonial administrator determined to stand no nonsense, the girl's features half-formed, malleable, with the kind of delicacy that is finally etched into characterful lines by some deep sexual relationship. 'I'm in love with Anthea. I think she is in love with me. We were – are – going away together. I'm trying to find her.' It was the truth, he thought, the truth as far as it went and as far as he knew it, although it omitted so much.

Rosemary Felton looked at him with melting eyes. 'That's terrible. I only just knew her myself, but that's just terrible, isn't it, Roger?'

'Just terrible,' Roger Sennett repeated with heavy irony. 'I don't know how to contain myself. That night in Pimlico was the first time you met her, wasn't it?'

'Yes.'

'Pretty quick decisions made on either side, weren't they?'

'Roger, don't be so cynical. I'm sorry,' she said to Hunter.

'You needn't apologise for somebody else's bad manners.' Hunter could feel the revolver, hard and comforting, in his hip pocket.

'He's not usually like this,' the girl assured him earnestly. 'But Anthea always has that kind of influence on people. I mean, an unsettling influence. She's that kind of girl.'

'Oh, shut up,' Sennett said. Abruptly he asked Hunter, 'How well do you know Anthea?'

'I don't know what you mean. I told you, we're in love with each other.'

'Christ, I'm not talking about that. You don't know what I'm talking about, do you?' Hunter shook his head. 'Put it this way. Did it surprise you that she was kidnapped?' Before he could answer this risible question,

Sennett went on, 'I wasn't surprised.'

'You weren't,' Hunter echoed. It seemed to him that this could mean only one thing, that Sennett knew of the kidnap plot.

'I knew something about the company she kept.'

He stupidly echoed again, 'The company she kept.'

'I see you don't know what I mean. I'd better tell you. At least, I suppose so. I never could tell whether I was doing right or wrong. The fact is, Anthea's had a pretty rough time. She's given other people a rough time, too.'

'What sort of rough time?'

Sennett filled their glasses again before he answered. 'She's been in a home.'

'In a home?'

'For drug addiction. Cocaine and marijuana mostly. Surely you realised – after all, you saw enough of her by your own account.'

The drops into depression, the nerves and fits of the jitters, the bright irresponsible gaiety and inability to concentrate, now they all clicked into place. And the things she had said about her stepfather, *I fool him, I do what I want*. 'I didn't realise,' he said. Something occurred to him and he said it, hesitantly yet with a sort of hopefulness. 'There were no marks. I mean, did she have injections?'

'Sometimes,' Sennett said gloomily. 'Where

the real addicts have them. Between the toes.' He leaned forward. Now that the thing had been said he talked eagerly, like a man anxious to vindicate himself.

'She came out eight months ago, supposed to be cured, and there was a sort of arrangement between my father and Moorhouse that I would look after her as much as I could. Go around with her, you know, make sure she didn't meet any undesirable acquaintances. Doesn't look as though I did very well, does it?'

'Roger, darling, you never told me that,' the girl said.

'Should I have done?' He frowned at the sherry glass in his hand, and did not look at Hunter. 'It was a hell of a job, I can tell you that. Don't know why I let myself in for it in the first place, except that I knew Anthea when we were both kids, as I told you, and liked her. She had a pretty ghastly time then. Really, she never got over her mother marrying again.'

'You knew her mother?'

'I used to go over the Manor and play with Anthea. She always wanted to play games about the theatre, pretending we were actor and actress. I thought it was pretty crazy then. I didn't know about her father.'

'Her father?' the girl said.

'He was a theatrical producer. She had a terrific thing about him. I thought she was a bit of a bore, I remember, but I felt sorry for her. She was a pinched, ugly little thing.'

'She is beautiful,' Hunter said.

'If you like that nervous, snorting, high-stepping type. Personally I'm not attracted.' Sennett put a hand on the girl's arm, and smiled at her.

'She told me about her father. And she said she ran away from home to join a circus.'

'That's right. There was a hell of a hulla-baloo. Reward, police search over six counties, that sort of thing. I didn't see her around that time, but I should guess she enjoyed it.'

'She told me that her stepfather...' He stopped. There seemed a kind of betrayal of Anthea in what he had been about to say.

'About him making a pass at her?' Rose-mary Felton gasped. 'Oh, yes, it's true.'

'True?'

'True that she said it, I mean. Whether it actually happened – how should I know? If you ask me I should guess that Anthea made it up. She's got a great imagination.' Rosemary Felton was wide-eyed.

'But it's an awful thing to say.'

'I dare say. Perhaps it didn't happen. I don't know. But it's no use blaming Anthea, blaming anybody, is it? It's the way we are that makes things happen to us.'

And what makes us the way we are,

Hunter thought? Aloud he said, 'When did she start to take drugs?'

Sennett shook his head. 'Don't know much about that, something to do with a jazz group she was mixed up with. She was having an affair, I think it was the trombonist, and I understand it was through him. But I don't know the details. Her stepfather had set her up in a flat and given her an allowance. Then the trombonist, or saxophonist, or whatever he was, left her, and from what I heard she really went haywire after that. Had what they call a nervous breakdown. After she took the cure he made her live at home, cut off her allowance, and I was called in. Doctor Sennett.' He laughed, not happily.

'Poor Anthea.' Rosemary Felton's eyes were filled with tears.

'Poor everybody. It's time we went to dinner.'

'Just another minute – five minutes,' Hunter said pleadingly. 'You say that's the story, but it's not quite the story. What about your looking after her, how did that work out?'

'I did what I could,' Sennett said defensively.

'But it didn't work out?'

'How the hell could it work out? I think she tried for a few weeks. After that she began to get drugs again. I knew she was getting them, but what could I do about it? If anyone wants to get drugs, they will.'

'Even without money?'

'I don't know where she got the money. Or how. I wouldn't like to guess.'

Hunter said nothing. Sennett got up, walked over to the mantelpiece, thumped his fist against it. 'You're going to say I might have done something, but what the hell could I do? Tell Moorhouse, and make her more unhappy than she was? I wouldn't do that. It's a bloody awful thing, I can tell you, when you can see somebody going down the slope and you know there's nothing you can do about it.'

Wasn't this what Hunter felt about himself, that he was going down the slope? But now he said, 'There's always something you can do about it. Anthea's in love with me.'

Somehow these words came out almost in the form of a question, but Sennett did not seem to notice it. He only said broodingly, 'She's been in love before. More than once.'

'What do you think has happened to her?'

'I don't know. This kidnapping stunt is just the crazy sort of idea she might think up herself to get money out of her father.' The shock of this remark transfixed Hunter for a moment. 'But I suppose that's not it. She wouldn't play it up this far. She must have got mixed up with another lot of dope peddlers, I suppose. That's what I meant when I said I know the company she keeps. When you really get tangled up with boys like that you can't tell how it will end, except that it's pretty certain to end badly.'

'Poor Anthea,' the girl said again. She added admiringly, 'You're hard, Roger.'

'It's life that's hard, not me. But I hope it's a long time before you have to find it out.' To Hunter he said abruptly. 'I don't know what you're looking for. I don't suppose I've been much help.'

'I'm looking for Anthea.'

'Are you?' Sennett's eyes, deep-set and dark, looked hard at him. 'I hope you're not disappointed when you find her.'

Chapter Twenty-nine

Eight o'clock. He had four hours in which to find Anthea, and to catch the plane for Tangier. But did he want to find her, now that the pattern of events had unfolded so far? *Anthea is in love with me.* Were the words true? Anthea has used me, he might as well have said, as a tool with which to pry money out of her father. She used me quite deliberately to get the money, and then who knows what she intended? Perhaps to use her part of it for buying drugs, perhaps to go abroad with me, steal the money, and then join her real lover, the man who supplied her with drugs for nothing. Was Bill Hunter, either way, conceivably anything more than a pawn in the game?

And if he could no longer honestly believe that Anthea was in love with him, had he ever been in love with Anthea? Was the feeling he had for her based on anything more than the fascination of sex, social position, the unknown? Against such rational arguments he could put only memories of Anthea as she had looked at and talked to him less than a week ago. Anthea in the white sleeveless frock at Richmond, showing him the den with a schoolgirl's pride, drawing on a stocking as she sat on the edge of the bed.

Such images persisted, and were stronger than rational argument. He stepped out of the cool dark evening into the synthetic warmth of a telephone box, and dialled Westmark's number.

Westmark answered on the first ring, and stopped Hunter as soon as he began to speak. 'Come over to see me, will you?'

'What's it all about? Has anything–'

'I said come over. I shall be expecting you.'

This time, the third time, the smell of luxury in the apartments caught in his throat. He could not separate his awareness of this smell from Westmark, who opened the door to him with a blank unsmiling face.

There was no sign of the Chinese girl.

Westmark did not offer Madeira. When they were in the great room that overlooked the Park he pointed to the rosewood table. The money was on it, stacked neatly in piles.

Hunter stared in bewilderment. 'I don't understand.'

'There is your money. You can take it away.'

'Why?'

'I asked if the money was hot. You said no. The money is hot.'

'What do you mean?'

'I do not take things on trust. I have a technician, an expert you might call him, who works on these things. Have you handled the money yourself? There is a stain on it that comes off on the hands.'

He looked down at his own hands. The fingertips were smudged with yellow. He tried without success to rub it off on his handkerchief. Westmark watched him with a kind of satisfaction.

'My man tells me that the stain is not injurious, it is some form of chemically-treated dust with which the notes have been impregnated. It will disappear from the fingers, he thinks, in a couple of days. Fortunately I have not handled the money myself.' He looked at his own fingers, plump and well-manicured, the cuticles pressed back.

'Is it all like this?'

'All that we have tested.'

So it had been as he guessed. Moorhouse had approached the police immediately. They had arranged to give him this money which would incriminate anybody who tried to get rid of it. Had there been a detective watching outside Knightsbridge station, a man who had followed them in, and to whom somehow Hunter had given the slip? That did not matter much now. The chemically-treated notes explained why no statement had been made public about the kidnap money. The police everywhere would have been notified to look out for the notes. Banks had no doubt been instructed to watch for them. The money was useless to him. It lay on the table there, money that looked green and fresh, and in fact was rotten.

'What are you waiting for?' Westmark's voice was harsh. 'I don't want it here. Take it away. There is a suitcase on the floor and a pair of gloves on the table.'

The suitcase was cheap, shiny, new. He snapped the lock of it open. 'How long does this dust last?' he asked the currency dealer.

'I've told you, on the hands perhaps two days.'

'And on the notes?'

'My man is not sure. Weeks, certainly. Perhaps months. I know what you are thinking. I will have nothing to do with it. Take the money away.'

'You've got places. You could keep the stuff until–'

'No.' Westmark looked at a wristwatch in which small diamonds glistened round the dial. 'I want you out of here in five minutes.'

He doesn't like it either, Hunter thought, the smell money has when it's gone rotten. He pulled on the gloves slowly, gloves deliciously soft and flexible, and began to pack away the money again in the shiny suitcase. Westmark watched in silence until he had put back half the packets. Then he said, 'You shouldn't have tried it, Hunter.'

His head jerked up. 'What?'

'I don't know what you have tried, and I don't want to know. But you won't do it. You're not made for it.'

The money was almost all in now. He dropped the last ten wads casually into the case, a mere matter of a thousand pounds, and closed it. 'I might as well burn the stuff,' he said viciously.

'Do as you wish. But you will not burn it here.' Westmark spoke slowly. 'As far as I am concerned I have not seen that money. It has never been in this apartment. You have never been here. Do you understand?'

'Yes.'

'I have my reputation to consider.' He relaxed suddenly, and became almost the old bland Westmark. 'Will you drink a glass of Madeira?'

'Thank you, no.'

'What are you going to do now?'

'I don't know,' he said, although he did know.

'You are not in need of any – of any money?' Westmark drew a gold-edged wallet from his pocket, opened it to reveal a large packet of notes, then began to laugh. Hunter laughed too. It was a good, though obvious joke.

The smell of money was with him all the way down in the lift. No doubt it came from the suitcase. It was not until he was out in the street that he remembered the peculiar concentration with which Crambo had looked at him. Hunter had thought the detective was looking at some mark on his clothing. He realised now that Crambo must have been looking at his hands.

Chapter Thirty

Eight-thirty. He went into a pub, and with a half pint of beer in front of him, sat down and tried to think. I have been stupid, he told himself, I have been unbelievably stupid all along. Was it too late to rectify that stupidity now? He looked down at the shiny new suitcase by his side, the suitcase filled with stinking money that was no use to him or to anybody, he looked at the faint pollen-like marks on his fingers, and he saw clearly enough the outline of the net that had almost closed over him.

Item, he said to himself, looking into the yellow depths of the golden beer that tasted like acid, whatever Anthea wanted or didn't want, whether I am right in believing that she loves me or whether she simply meant to use me as a tool, she wanted to get hold of this money. Therefore she meant to meet me at the den. Since she did not come there, she must have been prevented from doing so.

Item, it is a reasonable assumption that the person who stopped her was connected with the fact that she obtained drugs. How did she get the drugs? What was the only thing that interested her according to her stepfather, the thing that occupied much of her time? The Patriotic Fellowship Circle. In some way she got the drugs through the Circle.

Item the last, Hunter said to himself as he emptied the beer. It is quite certain that Crambo noticed those marks on my fingers. Why didn't he arrest me there and then? Because he expected me to lead him to the money, the money that lies stinking now at my feet. As soon as I left him he will have put a man on to follow me. This man – will there be one man or two? – will now be on the telephone asking for instructions, telling Crambo that I went into Westmark's apartment empty-handed and came out with a suitcase.

He picked up the suitcase, walked to the bar. 'Is there another way out of here?'

The barmaid gaped at him. 'What?'

'Another way out. There's a friend I don't want to miss. He may be in another bar.'

'There's the public, through that door.'

He walked through the door that led into the public bar, across that bar and out. An inconspicuous man in a grey raincoat stood by the kerb. He advanced and said, 'Excuse me, have you got a light?'

Hunter swung the suitcase up at the man's chest. Even as he did so he had a vivid image of the case bursting open and the wads of money being scattered all over the road as in some old French film. But he was lucky. The lock of the suitcase held as the edge of it, with the impact of an uppercut looped up from the floor, caught the man on the chin. He gave an inarticulate cry in which the two ingredients were evidently rage and surprise, and fell backwards. Hunter, still holding the suitcase, ran down an alley by the side of the pub.

Chapter Thirty-one

It was symptomatic, no doubt – but of precisely what? – that he should dive underground for security, as now he clattered down the steps of Hyde Park tube station. The backward look for a pursuer, the somehow furtive passage through the barrier, the quick run down the moving staircase, he had done all these or something very much like them before, and now as before nobody followed him, so that the whole tale of drugs and stolen money and Anthea's disappearance might have been part of some fantastic dream. The suitcase in his hand, however, like some compromising prop in a farce, the pair of knickers left on a chair in the drawing room, was a reminder that the dream was reality. Should he leave the suitcase in the Underground train? Somehow he found himself unable to do so. The money was useless, no doubt, yet it seemed to be the only thing, now, that bound him to the image of Anthea as it receded into the distance. To abandon the suitcase would be to admit that the image of Anthea had never been real.

He travelled for two stations, got out at Piccadilly Circus, walked down Lower

Regent Street and turned off it. The brass plate said PFC 1st Floor, but it was not this that he was looking for now. The plate he wanted was a dingy one low down on the other side of the door. It said, 'Caretaker. Night Only. Please Press'.

Hunter pressed the bell. There was no sound within the dark building. He pressed it again, and the door opened. A little old man with a four-day growth of beard peered at him.

'No good ringing like that. I got to come up from the basement and I have to take my time. Not so young as I was, you know.'

Which of us is, Hunter thought. Hunter tapped the suitcase. 'I've got some stuff here for the PFC. They told me it would be all right if I brought it along and saw you. I'm sorry to trouble you at this time of night.' He put his hand into his pocket, and then, when the caretaker's look of disapproval did not change, into his wallet.

At the sight of the note the old man's face changed as though a light had gone on inside it. 'You're a gentleman,' he said with apparent deep feeling. 'Bless you, sir, you're a gentleman.' What would he have said, Hunter wondered, how impossibly refulgent would his features have become, at sight of the suitcase's contents? 'You'd be a friend of Mr Pine, I expect. A real gentleman, Mr Pine, one of the old sort.'

'That's right. He has quite a few friends coming up here, I suppose.'

'A few. I wouldn't say a lot.'

'And Miss Moorhouse? She comes up too, I expect.'

The little eyes peering at him were slightly suspicious now, the voice's whine sharpened a little in tone. 'You've got your key.'

If I say no he won't let me go up, Hunter thought. 'Yes.'

'Shut this front door when you go out. I'd come up with you, but I got to look after the boilers.' The caretaker shuffled away, and disappeared in the darkness of the passage. Hunter went up the stairs.

It is hardly possible to spend ten months in prison, let alone ten years, without learning how to pick simple locks. The lock of the glass entrance door was of the kind that can be opened with a thin piece of wire. Hunter managed it with the aid of two bent paper clips which he found in his pockets.

The cover was over the typewriter in the outer office. Hunter glanced at the filing cabinet, rejected it as too public a repository for secrets, and opened the door lettered in gold, *Mr H A Pine*. He entered a small room with a carpet, a desk, a hatstand, a cupboard. The cupboard contained stationery, pencils, a hand printing machine at which he glanced briefly. The desk, then? It was a standard type of kneehole desk in light oak, with 'In' and 'Out' trays filled with papers, a clean blotter, an engagement pad, a tube of Alka Seltzer, and a bottle containing a well-known brand of health salts guaranteed to give, as the advertisements put it, a beneficial shake-up to the whole system.

The engagement pad did not mention Anthea Moorhouse's name, nor even her initials. The engagements listed over the past two weeks seemed to consist of occasions at which Pine had spoken, or had taken the chair. There were one or two notes like: 'Lunch Blake 1.0. Discuss Rhodesian trip. Travers and Johnson evening. Drinks and dinner. Possibilities New Zealand development.' He looked quickly through the papers in the trays. Arrangements for meetings, trips, discussions, answers to inquiries about the objects of the PFC. Nothing which indicated that Pine was anything but what he appeared to be, a busy man concerned with preserving the bonds of Empire. He tried the drawers of the desk. Three on each side were open, and contained what seemed to be perfectly innocent papers and memoranda. The fourth drawer on each side was locked. These drawers would have to be forced.

He tried his own pen knife, broke the blade of it, and looked round for a chisel or a screwdriver. But the PFC had apparently no chisels or screwdrivers for the assistance of burglars. He went back into the outer office and then into Rawlinson's room, which was a slightly larger version of Pine's. There was no chisel or screwdriver here, but in one of the cupboards he found an old file, which tapered to a point.

He tried without success to insert this file in the slight gap between the top of the desk and the locked drawer. There was a small single steel filing cabinet in the outer office, and he used this as a very inadequate hammer. At last he was able to force the file between the two pieces of wood. After that it was only a matter of time, while he worked at the wood round the lock. When he had the file right inside he levered on it. For a moment he was afraid that the file would break. Then there was a tearing sound, and the wood round the lock gave way.

He opened the drawer, and stared disbelievingly at its contents. There were some twenty little envelopes in the drawer, of the kind used as wage packets. He picked up the envelopes one by one, and examined them. They were exactly what they appeared to be, and they were empty.

Hunter looked at the other drawer, and wondered whether there was any point in forcing it. A man who kept empty wage packets in one locked drawer might keep a ready reckoner in the other. But why, then, did friends of Pine's come up to this office in the evening? He began to work on the other drawer.

Five minutes later he had it open, and he began to laugh. The drawer contained two more tubes of Alka Seltzer and two more jars of health salts. There were also some papers. They contained lists of some two hundred and fifty names and addresses, headed, 'Regular Monthly Contributors to PFC Funds.' Most of the names were of women, and some of them were titled.

Hunter stopped laughing. He wondered why a man should want to keep so many bottles of Alka Seltzer and health salts in his office, and why he should keep them under lock and key. There was a wash basin in the room, with a plastic mug by its side. He put water in the mug, shook some of the powder from the jar of health salts on the desk into it. The mixture fizzed like health salts, and tasted like health salts. He repeated the operation with powder from both jars in the drawer. It did not fizz. He emptied out the water and put the white powder on his tongue. It tasted bitter.

He repeated the test with the Alka Seltzer tablets, which in every case fizzed, and bounced up to the surface. The Alka Seltzer was genuine.

The outer office contained a telephone directory. In the L–R section he found Pine, H A, 34 Mallorby Gardens, SW7.

Hunter put the two jars containing drugs

into his pocket. He picked up the suitcase, went down the stairs and out, without seeing the caretaker. He closed the door of the office block behind him. As he turned again into Lower Regent Street, his face was solemn.

Chapter Thirty-two

Nine-fifteen. As he walked up Mallorby Gardens, which led off a South Kensington square, the rain fell again on his shoulders, gentle as feathers. The road was a Regency terrace, the houses elegant and elongated, decayed but smart. There were neat wrought-iron balconies on the first floors, some of them containing pots from which creepers trailed ornamentally about. The doors had been painted in different bright colours. Hunter trudged up the road regardless of the rain, a man set in some sort of obscure dream like a fly in jelly, the suitcase heavy at his side. He said aloud, 'Twenty-six, twenty-eight, thirty.' Then he stopped in surprise.

The door of number thirty-four Mallorby Gardens stood open. From inside the house came the steady but not furious buzz of voices which indicates that a party is going on. There were occasional bursts of laughter. Shadow people moved against the ground floor curtains. Like all group activities this party, with its lights and dynamic hum of conversation, produced an impression of gaiety and unity almost unbearable to those left outside it. On the steps Hunter paused, overwhelmed by his own loneliness, appalled that he was about to force this loneliness and sense of loss upon those within. Then he walked up the steps and through the open door into a long narrow hall. A stairway faced him. From rooms on his left he heard voices, less agreeable now that they could be individually distinguished.

The door of the nearest room opened, and a coffee-coloured young man came out. He wore a yellow pullover, tight grey corduroy trousers and plum-coloured suede shoes. His eyes were brilliant.

'Welcome to the Circle,' he said. 'May the bonds of our Empire grow even stronger.' He extended his hand and, when Hunter took it, attempted to shake hands so that their fingers interlaced. He looked surprised at Hunter's resistance. 'You do not know the Brothers' Grip?'

'I want to see Mr Pine.'

'You are a new Link. Come in.'

His companion turned, and entered the room on the left. Hunter saw a cupboard, opened it, and pushed the shiny suitcase among the brooms and carpet sweeper inside. Then he closed the cupboard door, and followed the young man.

Inside the room, the crowd swayed like that in an Underground train during the rush hour. Many of them were in, or just out of, their teens, and they fell into easily definable groups, eager and serious students from the Colonies, other Colonial students of a more raffish kind like the one who had just spoken to Hunter, and the English varieties he had already seen at the meeting, scoutmasters, Blimps, scorbutic young men. In one corner, near the window, a group of Chinese stood, grave and quiet. Nearer to him an Indian with gold-rimmed spectacles was arguing with one of the scorbutic young men. Standing on tiptoe Hunter saw through an archway a further room crowded with people. Beyond them he glimpsed a bar. He looked round hopefully for Anthea, but could not see. Nor could he see Pine or Rawlinson, or even the coffee-coloured young man in the yellow pullover.

'Mountbatten was England's saviour,' the Indian with gold-rimmed spectacles said. 'Without Mountbatten, with one of your old Imperialist Viceroys, today India would have broken away. A link in the chain would be broken.'

'You're talking rot, old boy,' the young Englishman said. His voice was loud and confident. Red pustules glowed angrily on his pale face. 'Trouble with you chaps is you disregard the whole course of Imperial history, just concentrate on the last few years. Nothing against Mountbatten personally, but he was the wrong man in the wrong place at the wrong time–'

Dear God, Hunter thought, have I come here to listen to this? He tried to move, and found his buttocks firmly pressed against those of a young Indian girl wearing a sari. She turned her head and looked coldly at him. Hunter said, 'Excuse me,' and tried to push, but the mass of bodies surrounding him appeared impermeable. Snatches of conversation, less intelligible the longer he listened, came from all about him.

'The Empire ideal is not the Imperialist ideal, you must realise that.'

'I am surprised to hear even an Englishman attempt to maintain the proposition that there was anything at all idealistic about Imperialism–'

That was Gold Rims, no doubt.

'You know the Fellowship slogan, forge the links and make the chain.'

'It is said also that the strength of a chain is the strength of its weakest link. At the moment that link is–'

'Admit the difficulties in South Africa, and you must still agree–'

'–a strong hand at the helm. That's what makes the difference between success and failure.'

'–what Disraeli was doing was–'

'–the Primrose League–'

'– don't forget that Disraeli was a Jew–'

'My dear, I thought I'd never make it,' a voice said. It was the young man in the yellow pullover, and he held a large glass filled with yellow liquid in his hand. It was an extremely innocuous cider cup.

'My name is Hassan,' the young man said.

'Yes. Are you Egyptian?'

'My father was Egyptian, but I come from Malaya. What is your name?'

'Hunter. Bill Hunter.' There was no longer any point in concealment. 'Do you know Miss Moorhouse?'

'I thought you wanted to see Arthur Pine.'

'I do, but I want to talk to Miss Moorhouse as well. Do you know her?'

'I think so,' Hassan said vaguely. 'Arthur – Mr Pine – is not here just now. He is engaged. We have these meetings every month, do you like them? They are to introduce new Links and old ones.'

'You said that before. What is a Link – a member?'

'Yes. Many Links make the chain,' Hassan said solemnly. 'And the complete chain makes the Circle. Every new Link learns the Brothers' Grip. I showed you before, like this.' He caught Hunter's hand and twined his fingers in it.

'I think I'd better have a look round. I

haven't got much time.'

'Hush.' Hassan looked at him sidewise. 'Later I will help you. Now we are to sing the Song of the Circle.'

Hassan took Hunter's right hand, and twined his fingers in the Brothers' Grip. At the same time his left hand was taken by the Indian with gold-rimmed spectacles. All over the room little circles were being formed by the interlaced hands. Except that their hands were not crossed, it was strongly reminiscent of Auld Lang Syne. Someone clapped, and Hunter saw through the archway the awkward figure of Mr Rawlinson bob up on what seemed to be an improvised platform. The Adam's apple moved up and down.

'We will now – ah – sing the Song of the Circle,' he said. Somebody put on a gramophone record and they followed the words, their voices ragged at first, but gathering strength and unity after a couple of lines. As they sang they moved round together slowly.

Workers of hand, workers of brain,
Forge the Links that make the Chain,
The Chain that with its Brothers' grip
Joins us in deepest Fellowship.

From deserts, islands, lands of gold,
Come black and white, come young and old,
To join hands in the Brother's grip
And sing of Empire Fellowship.

At one side of him Hassan sang the words with deep feeling. On the other the Indian seemed under the impression that he was singing a dirge. There were several verses, and Hunter found his attention wandering after four or five of them. At the other end of the room, beyond the archway, there was some sort of movement. For a moment he saw in the doorway the thin, nervous, handsome face of Pine. This face looked rapidly round the room as if in search of something or somebody, the lips moving. Then it was withdrawn.

In the next moment he saw Anthea. She was in one of the circles in the other room, near Rawlinson. She was wearing a green frock, cut low at the back. He glimpsed her profile, classic and severe, and then the movement of the circles hid her from him. He tried to break out of his own circle but Hassan and the Indian held their fingers tightly laced with his. Hassan gave him one reproachful glance, shook his head slightly, and went on singing. When at last the song was over, he spoke.

'You must not break the Circle, it is strictly forbidden. It means you are a weak Link.'

'If you will excuse me,' the Indian said politely, 'I should like to discuss with you the question of the Empire. Are you of the opinion that the best way to preserve the bonds of Empire is by absolute possibility of self-determination for all peoples?'

'Some other time,' Hunter said. 'I must just talk to someone.'

He pushed his way across the room, after Anthea in her green dress. It was like trying to move through a sea of flesh. Impermeable bodies and the faces attached to them, black, yellow, pinkish, nodding like flowers on their stalks, barred his way. Beneath the continual babble of sound he tried to order his own thoughts, to understand the meaning of Anthea's presence. Noise can intoxicate, in its different way, as much as drink, and his head was fuzzy with it. 'Mr Smith,' a voice said, as at last he reached the archway, 'I say, Mr Smith.'

A hand grasped his arm. He turned his head. Rawlinson's face, the false teeth in full grin, was inches from his own. 'How delightful to see you, Mr Smith,' he said.

'You'll have to excuse me. I'm looking for Miss Moorhouse.'

Rawlinson stood directly in front of him now, blocking his path. 'Always extremely glad to see new faces. This is one of the get-togethers I told you about, if you remember. Have you signed the Bond?'

Hunter tried desperately to look beyond him. 'Miss Moorhouse was quite close to you during the song. You must have seen her.'

Among the noise of voices, it seemed really impossible to make verbal contact. Rawlinson now, with his smile fixed like the grin on a skull, said, 'The Bond is for every new Link. In it you agree to do your level best to strengthen the ties of Empire–'

Hunter took Rawlinson by the arm and shook him slightly. 'Anthea Moorhouse. Where is she?'

Rawlinson's eyes protruded like those of a fish. 'Miss Moorhouse? Why, I haven't seen her.'

Hunter pushed him away. Now the once-impermeable crowds seemed to melt under the glow of his anger, so that it was suddenly easy to get across to the bar. But where was Anthea? Hunter saw her in the green dress with her back to him, standing near the door. Anger spurted in him again, anger that she should have so utterly deceived him. He walked over, placed his hand on her bare shoulder and spun her round, saying harshly, 'Anthea.'

The girl in the green dress stared at him. She was not Anthea, she was not even like Anthea, now that he saw her full face. There was a similarity of profile, nothing more. The girl's face was red with annoyance. She raised her hand and struck Hunter on the cheek. He mumbled something, inarticulate words of apology, and turned away to face, on a level well below his own, the china blue eyes of Tanya Broderick.

In her precise little voice she said, 'You newspapermen really do get around, don't you? Where's your friend?'

'He's working this evening.'

'Finding the vital witness? Such a funny man with that long nose.' Her voice mocked him openly. Tonight she wore a frock the colour of her eyes, and her nails also were enamelled blue. The shoes she wore were like stilts, but even so she hardly came up to his shoulder.

'What are you doing here?' Hunter asked. 'You don't mean to tell me you're a Link.'

'Of course.' She giggled and then looked serious. 'But you're not. What are *you* doing here, I should like to know. What do you want?'

'I'm here to find a girl named Anthea Moorhouse.'

'You're a bit behind the times. She's been kidnapped.'

'I read that. I want to talk to Pine.'

'She has been kidnapped, hasn't she? If you know anything about it, tell me.' The anxiety in her voice puzzled him.

'That's what the papers say. But I believe Pine knows something about it.'

'Why should he know anything? Anyway, she's not here.' Now the anxiety in her voice was unmistakable. 'You'd better get out.'

'I'll go after I've talked to Pine.'

'You're out to make trouble, I can see that. You're no more a newspaperman than you're my Aunt Fanny. Don't think you ever fooled me. Not for a minute you didn't.'

'You're very smart. But I still want to see Pine.'

'You do? I'll tell you something. You're a fool.'

She was turning away when Hassan's voice said, 'Excuse me. Am I an interruption?'

Hunter said, 'Why no, Hassan. I'm glad to see you.' The boy looked at him, and then began to giggle. 'Please forgive me, Mr Hunter. It looked very funny, although I am sure embarrassing.'

'What was that?'

'The little incident a minute or two ago. You made a certain suggestion, as English newspapers say, and it was repulsed.'

'That's not the way it was at all.'

'Ah, no. I am only saying what appeared, if you understand me. I know that is not the case, because you are my friend, Mr Hunter. I wish to help you.'

'Then can you find Miss Moorhouse?'

'I have not seen her this evening. But I think I can help you to find Mr Pine. That will do just as well, if you understand me.' Hassan giggled again. 'Come with me.'

They went out of the door again into the passage. Hassan led the way upstairs.

Chapter Thirty-three

Upstairs the roar of the party was subdued again, as it had been from outside. Hassan led the way to the back of the house, tapped gently on a white door, and opened it.

They entered a sitting room with sofa and armchairs, shabby but comfortable. There was a door leading out of it, presumably to a bedroom. The room was dimly lighted by a standard lamp, but Hunter saw the range of gleaming silver cups on the mantelpiece. Beneath the lamp Pine sat in an armchair, his head back and his eyes closed.

Hassan closed the door softly behind him. When he spoke he was restraining a giggle. 'I have brought up a friend of mine, Arthur. He wanted to see Anthea, but I told him you would do just as well.'

Pine opened his eyes. He seemed to have difficulty in focusing them, and his voice was thick. 'What?'

'A very good friend of mine, Mr Bill Hunter,' Hassan said.

Now Pine's eyes focused. He looked at Hunter with a stare which, for a moment, held pure terror. He said to Hassan, 'You brought this man up here?'

Hassan looked from one to the other of them. 'Was it wrong? He is not–'

'You've done nothing wrong,' Hunter said. 'I'd have got to see him, with your help or without it. We've got a little business to settle.'

Hassan ignored him. 'Arthur,' he said questioningly, and moved lightly across the room to the chair. 'Arthur.'

Pine struggled up, like a man swimming upwards through water. 'It's done now. You'd better leave us alone.'

'But is he–' Hassan left the sentence uncompleted.

'I'm not from the police, if that's what's worrying you,' Hunter said. 'Now get out.'

'Arthur, please tell me that I have not done wrong.' Hassan's voice was pleading.

'You couldn't help it. And now, you heard what he said. Leave us alone.'

Hassan went out and closed the door. Before closing it he spoke two monosyllables to Hunter.

Pine got out of the chair now, stood up, walked over to the mantelpiece. He gestured at the cups behind him. 'Looking at these? Sporting trophies. Used to be a sprinter five years ago. Just a little out of condition.'

Now Hunter saw photographs on the walls too, Pine breasting the tape, receiving cups from vaguely-recognisable dignitaries. He said nothing.

'Didn't understand that remark of yours about the police,' Pine said. 'What the devil did it mean?'

'It's simple enough. If I hadn't been stupid I'd have understood it long ago. You're part of a drug ring. You distribute drugs with that crackpot PFC as a cover. Anthea's an addict and she helps with the distribution, which is always the difficult part for people running drugs. She acts as distributor by a simple but ingenious method. Rawlinson pretty well told me what it was when I came to see you in the office.

'The PFC has a list of people who make regular contributions to its funds, and they make these contributions when Anthea calls on them. At the same time she delivers their supplies. For doing this Anthea gets her own drugs for nothing, and you also give her money. No doubt you've got other agents doing the same thing, as well as boys like Hassan. The drill is that the agents call at the office to collect supplies. They have a key to one side of the desk. There they find packets sealed up ready for delivery. They look like little wage packets, and I suppose in a way that's just what they are.'

Pine's face was pale. The tic worked in his cheek. 'I don't know what you're talking about.'

Hunter took the two health salts bottles out of his pocket. Pine sucked in his breath, held out a hand and drew it back. In a voice that, absurdly, sounded indignant, he said, 'You've burgled the office.'

'Let me make this clear. I'm not interested in these bottles. I'm not interested in you. I want to find Anthea.'

The shot Pine had taken before Hunter's arrival was taking effect. Standing with his back to those brightly-shining cups he said almost gaily, 'I only know what I read in the evening papers. Anthea appears to have been kidnapped. Hadn't you seen? But perhaps you've stopped reading the papers since that business about Bond. Reading the papers can get you into trouble.'

'Where is she?'

'I really have no idea.'

Hunter felt the initiative slipping away from him. 'She came into the PFC office and saw you on that Monday morning. I know that.'

'Why shouldn't you know it? The police do, too. Anthea came in, asked about doing some more canvassing, and left. That's what I told the police, and as far as I'm concerned anybody else is welcome to know it too.' Now Pine was mocking him openly. 'You forget, Hunter, that I'm a respectable man. I used to run for England. People forget athletes quickly, but they haven't forgotten me yet. I'm not a convicted criminal.'

'You know who I am,' Hunter said slowly.

'You knew me when I came into the office that day. What else do you know about Anthea and me?'

Pine shrugged his thin shoulders. 'When Anthea's a little high she'll tell anybody anything. Or when she's low and in need of a shot. She isn't a girl to keep secrets. And perhaps I ought to say, so that you and I know where we are, that she isn't a one-man girl either.'

Behind Pine's mockery Hunter detected some sort of insecurity. What was its cause? 'Did she tell you what she was going to do?'

'She told me that she was coming into money, a lot of it. Would that be news to you, now? I doubt it. And where would Anthea get a lot of money. Could it be from her stepfather?' Pine seemed to cut himself off in mid-speech, as though conscious of having said too much. From somewhere, perhaps from outside, came a noise closer than the hum below. It might have been the sound of a foot scraping on the floor.

But had Pine said too much by revealing that he knew something about the kidnap plot? What did it matter, after all, when he could not find Anthea? Wearily, he got up to go. Pine faced him with a smile that was belied by the tic working in his cheek.

'Monday morning at your office was the last time you saw Anthea, then?'

'Of course.' Pine put up his hand to hide

the tic.

It was as he turned away from Pine that he saw, placed carelessly between two of the cups, the spectacles, the blue-rimmed spectacles with ornamental edges that Anthea had worn for the passport photograph.

He turned back to Pine, and there must have been something frightening in his look as he said, 'Where is she?'

The thin man backed away from the mantelpiece, across the room. 'I told you, I don't know.'

'Those are her spectacles. She has been here since Monday morning. She's here now.'

'No.'

'You've got her in there.' Hunter pointed to the inner door. 'I heard a noise.'

'No.' Pine was cringing now. Hunter went over, took him by the neck, twisted his arm. The arm was thin and brittle, like a stick.

'Oh, please,' Pine said, and said it again. 'Oh, please. You're hurting me.'

'Go and open that door.'

'It's no use. Don't be so beastly. Anthea's not in there.'

Hunter flung Pine aside hard, so that he knocked over a chair and lay on the floor, whimpering a little. He walked over to the inner door and opened it. A man was standing there waiting for him, a man who held a gun in his right hand. He looked hard and long at the man's face and felt the dark gigantic shadow of the past, a shadow stretching farther back than he would have believed possible, spread over him like a shroud.

Chapter Thirty-four

The name, on his lips, was like the answer to a riddle. 'Brannigan.'

The square face, strong and vicious, the cropped light hair above it, had not changed very much. Experience had put some lines into a face that had been smooth. The face was fatter, the mouth thinner. In the grey eyes there had been, twenty years ago, some glimmer of light – the light of idealism, of belief in something. Or was that merely a sentimental invention about the past? Certainly there was no such light in the eyes that looked steadily at him now.

'Bill O'Brien,' Brannigan said. He had always been proud of the fact that his voice showed little emotion, Hunter remembered. Now it lacked any kind of emphasis or colour. It was the voice one would expect to hear from a robot.

'Get back into the room, Bill.' Before the gun, Hunter moved backwards. 'Sit down,'

Brannigan said, and he sat in one of the armchairs. Pine scrambled up, picked up the blue-rimmed spectacles and dropped them in his pocket. Then he stood again with his back to the mantelpiece.

'I told you to be careful,' Brannigan said to Pine. Although the words were colourless Pine flinched as though he had been burned. Brannigan spoke to Hunter with the same mildness. 'You've caused a lot of trouble, Bill.'

Looking at him Hunter did not see the present Brannigan, a puffy snake in a well-cut dark suit. Twenty years had, after all, made some differences. He remembered the hard young IRA captain of long ago giving orders to the three of them, and giving the orders in a way that showed clearly enough his contempt for the human material he was using. He had known long ago, listening to Brannigan in a little candle-lit room, that the man giving them orders did not care whether they lived or died so long as they carried out the job. He relived the moment in which the smoke rose from his revolver and the night watchman, that old man with the ridiculous name, half turned round slowly and then fell down, crumpling from the knees like a doll.

'You work for Mekles,' he said. 'You told him about my record, and my real name.'

'That's right, Bill.' The gun in Brannigan's

hand did not waver. 'The governor had the idea that he wanted to appear on this programme. I thought it was a bad idea, but it was what he wanted. I was able to give him a little information about you. He always likes to have a little information about the people he's working with. Not that he uses it unless he has to. You made him use it.'

'It was an accident.'

'That was unlucky. For you, I mean. If what you're saying is true.'

'It is true.'

Brannigan shrugged. 'Not that it matters either way, though it was a nuisance at the time. Bond was one of our boys and he'd begun to fiddle, trying to keep a percentage for himself over and above the cut we gave him. I told him he was finished, his supplies would be cut off. He wouldn't believe it, got on the line to the governor, talked to him. When he learned it was so he jumped out of the window.'

'I didn't know anything about that. I was just firing a shot in the dark.'

'That was your bad luck,' Brannigan said again. He did not trouble to imply belief or disbelief.

'But he didn't jump. He was pushed. You pushed him.'

'Can you prove that?'

'You planted a witness in the block of flats

opposite, and she said what you told her to say. You talked to her on the telephone when I was in her flat. Tanya Broderick.'

'Did I talk to her? Tanya's a respectable girl. For that matter I'm respectable too. I don't think you're saying anything, Bill.'

'I should have paid more attention when I was told that you worked for Mekles. At the time it didn't seem important.' Brannigan nodded in acknowledgement of this remark. 'Have you been working for him long?'

'Long enough to get used to it.'

'You've come a long way from Dublin, Paddy.'

'It's not only a long way. It's a long time.' Brannigan seemed to be waiting for an answer, or perhaps another question. When Hunter said nothing he went on talking in his soft, cold voice. 'You won't find Anthea here. Only her spectacles.'

'Where is she?'

'She's dead, Bill. She's been dead since Monday. Strangled. Down in the cellar.'

Although Hunter knew that Brannigan would not hesitate to lie, he felt no doubt that this was the truth. If he had had any doubt it would have been cancelled by Pine's gasp of terror.

'Don't be a fool,' Brannigan said contemptuously to Pine. 'You've nothing to worry about. He killed her.'

'I don't see–' Pine said, and broke down in

a stutter.

'It's obvious enough. Anthea had a key to this house, isn't that right? Sometimes she used to meet Bill O'Brien, or Hunter, or whatever he calls himself here. They arranged this crazy kidnap idea together, but Hunter was double-crossing her, planning to kill her when they had the money. He wouldn't go shares, you see. He was greedy.'

'You can never make it stick,' Hunter said.

'Why not? Anthea took drugs. She kept a stock of them here. Pine trusted her too much. He's a bit of a fool, not too strong in the head, all his sense used to be in his feet when he was a runner. But then, why shouldn't he trust her? After all, she was the chairman's stepdaughter. And then there's the money. You've got the money, haven't you, Bill?'

'Why did I come back here?'

'You were afraid that Pine had found out something that would betray you.'

'It will be my word against his.'

'And which do you think will be believed?' Pine had recovered his spirits, he was almost jaunty. 'I don't think there's any question about *that*.'

'It won't be your word against anybody's, Bill.' Brannigan's voice was flat, disinterested. 'You've come to the end of the line.'

His mouth was dry. He could see no purpose in talk, yet he felt it necessary to go on talking. 'What do you mean?'

'Pine found Anthea's body. You wore gloves when you strangled her by the way. He accused you when you came here, you attacked him, he had to shoot you. Self-defence.'

'You bloody murderer,' Hunter said. He thought not of himself but of Anthea, the beautiful face blackened in death, the tongue lolling, bitten.

'I had nothing to do with it.' Pine cried the words as though they were some sort of invocation. Hunter took a step forward.

'Don't do it,' Brannigan said. 'I don't want to shoot now, but if you make me I will.'

'You say you're going to shoot anyway. Supposing I take the chance?'

'You know me too well to take that sort of chance,' Brannigan said in his flat voice. He spoke to Pine. 'How soon can you get that rabble out of here?'

'In half an hour they'll be gone. Perhaps less.'

'You've got that long, Bill. Something may happen in the next half hour, that's what you'll think. It won't, but you'll still hope. I know you, Bill.'

You know me too well, Hunter thought, feeling the gun in his hip pocket, so well that you don't even bother to search me. If he could distract Brannigan's attention, get him to turn round, he would have time to profit by this overconfidence. Meanwhile he had to go on talking.

'Supposing I hadn't come here. What would you have done then?'

'I wish you hadn't come. There's always a risk in gunplay. I don't like it. You'd have been picked up sooner or later, identified as the man mixed up in this plot of Anthea's, and we'd have taken it from there. That would have been better. But we can't leave it at that now, you know too much. You were a dead duck, though, as soon as you got mixed up with that crazy plot of Anthea's.' With mild reproof Brannigan said, 'That was a silly thing to do.'

Hunter said, genuinely puzzled, 'You knew about the idea from the beginning, then?'

'A girl like Anthea, how could you expect her to keep anything to herself?'

'I didn't know she was an addict.'

'You didn't know much.' Brannigan threw his revolver up in the air, caught it as it came down, laughed at Hunter's involuntary movement. He's too quick for me, Hunter thought despairingly, he's a gunman and I shall need seconds to get my revolver out. 'You knew she had Pine as her second string boyfriend? No? As I say, you didn't know much. She told him the idea six months ago, get money from the old man and live happily ever after somewhere out of this world. Pine's a fool, but he wasn't stupid enough to buy that one. You were. Even if you'd got away with the money, how long do you suppose she'd have stayed with you?'

'She loved me.' Even as Hunter spoke the words he knew that they were meaningless to Brannigan. And sure enough he ignored them. 'Go down and send them home,' he said to Pine. 'We can't wait all night.'

'Rawlinson's really in charge. It won't be long now before they've gone. I don't think I'd better–' His voice died away.

'Rawlinson's honest, I suppose,' Hunter said.

Brannigan laughed contemptuously. 'He doesn't know whether he's coming or going.'

'You've no right to talk like that about Rawlinson,' Pine said hotly. 'He believes in the Circle. He thinks it's doing good.'

'You give him a helping hand, I must say.' The words were ironical, but there was no irony in Brannigan's way of delivering them. It was as though he were beyond irony, as he was beyond hope, pleasure, sorrow, or anything except the mechanical actions that made up his life. 'But to hell with Rawlinson. It's your house, isn't it? Get them out.'

The tic in Pine's face had come back. 'You're not going to–'

'Don't worry. I shan't do anything until they've gone, unless Bill here makes me, and he won't do that. Afterwards you can stuff cotton wool in your ears.' Pine went out. Watching Hunter, Brannigan said, 'You couldn't get away with the money, because they sprayed some sort of chemical on it.'

Hunter had thought himself beyond surprise. 'How did you know that?'

'Here's the way it went. First, Pine sees that Anthea's very excited about something or other. She's bursting to tell him about it, finally can't stop herself, says she's found somebody else with more guts than Pine, who's going to carry out her wonderful kidnap plan.

'Now, Pine's fond of Anthea, fonder than he is of anything except coke. Doesn't want to lose her. He tries to talk her out of it. Doesn't have any luck. Anthea finally gets angry, tells him she's sick of the PFC racket anyway, and when this plan goes through she's going to have enough money to get her own supplies. All right. If she's that crazy, let her try it. But Pine's jealous, threatens to cut off her supplies here and now, unless she gives up the plan and stops seeing you. Then Anthea says something else. She says she doesn't like the way we've been fooling her old man – her old man, mark you, who isn't really her old man at all, and who's kept her without money ever since she came out of the bin – and she may decide to sing about the whole PFC racket. When she says that, Pine comes to me.'

Hunter felt a rush of pity for Anthea, a full realisation of how she had been trapped by her own temperament. In his mind there was an image of a bird with limed wings, struggling to fly. 'Why to you?' he said to Anthea's murderer. 'Why should Pine come to you?'

'The governor – Mekles – put me in charge of things over here when we found out that there was trouble with Bond. He doesn't like people who cause trouble. He doesn't like them in or near the organisation. He was really upset about that television business. So Pine came to me because it was trouble. And I decided that we couldn't afford that sort of trouble. Anthea had to go.'

Anthea had to go. It was as simple as that. For Brannigan it had always been as simple as that.

'Anthea had told Pine what she was planning. That meant she was already working with somebody, so I put a tail on her to find out who it was. And what did we turn up but you. That really was a joke.' Brannigan did not laugh. Downstairs voices could be heard in the street. People were saying goodbye. There was not much time left. 'The perfect setup. A previous murder conviction, not much money. You must have been crazy.'

Brannigan strolled across the room to a table on which a record player stood. He lifted the lid, put it on, listened for a moment to a recording of 'The Double You Blues':

'I've got those double you blues.
One of you is kind and one of you is not.
One of you's cold and one of you's hot.
Those double you blues–'

He nodded, took it off again.

'You killed her.'

'That's right. She went to the office to get some stuff from Pine. She was on tea, and wanted to stock up before starting out on her little adventure with you. Pine said he hadn't got any stuff at the office, and told her to come here. She had a key to the place already, of course.'

'And when she got here she found you.'

'That's right.' Brannigan took out a packet of cigarettes, put one between his lips, lighted it, all with one hand. The other hand still held the revolver. He threw the packet over to Hunter. 'Smoke?'

'Pine can't like the idea of her being found here.'

'No.' Brannigan blew a smoke ring. 'But he has to take it. He's too frightened to do anything else. And anyway, the PFC is expendable. It's clumsy. We've got to reorganise, as I told the governor. Hairdressers, manicurists, that's the thing.'

The voices downstairs had died away. Hunter moved in the chair so that he could more readily reach the revolver at his hip, but he knew that it was hopeless, that Brannigan would be too fast for him. 'How did you know about the money?'

'You were going abroad, it was a cinch you'd try to get rid of it. I got in touch with the two or three boys who run currency fiddles, Morgan, Westmark, Dawes. I told them to let me know as soon as anything came through, and to make it good when they dealt with you. They know Mekles, they like to oblige him.' Brannigan looked at Hunter as if he were an insect. 'You never had a chance. You must see it.'

From below Rawlinson's voice could be heard faintly, saying goodbye. Brannigan stubbed out his cigarette. The door opened and Pine stood there, his face the colour of cream cheese.

'They've gone.' His voice was high.

Brannigan lifted the lid of the record player, then closed it again.

There were footsteps on the stairs.

'Who's that?' Brannigan asked.

Pine was stammering again. 'I don't know. I felt sure everyone had gone.' He turned the handle of the door and said with relief, 'It's only Tanya.'

Tanya Broderick was smoking a cigarette in a jewelled blue holder. She stood in the doorway looking at the revolver in Brannigan's hand.

'You'd better get out of here.' The Irishman's voice was conversational, even.

She took out the cigarette, stubbed it in an ashtray, put away the holder. 'You're going to kill him. Who is he?'

'His name's Hunter, and he's mixed up with Anthea Moorhouse.'

'He was one of those two who came to see me.'

'I know that.'

'Where is she, Paddy? Where is Anthea Moorhouse?'

Pine said in his high voice, 'You read the papers, you know as much as we do. She's been kidnapped.'

'That's not what he thinks. I believe she's dead.'

'Really now, Tanya, you're being silly.'

'Let's cut out the nonsense,' Brannigan said. 'Yes, kid, she's dead. What are you going to do about it?' The revolver in his hand was still pointed at Hunter.

'Oh, my God. I wish I'd never started this.' She looked unseeingly at Hunter, her doll-face crumpled. Out of the eyes rolled two round tears.

'I like you, kid. Don't tell me you're going soft.'

'I hate you,' she said to Brannigan. 'You've tricked me. When you put me in that flat you said you were taking it for me.'

'So I was, kid. So I was taking it for you.'

'You took it so that I could swear I saw him jump. I didn't know what I was doing. You told me it was just to avoid awkward questions over a business deal. I never knew you killed him.'

'Who's saying I killed him, kid?' Brannigan's voice was low and level, but Hunter could feel the tension behind it.

Her own voice had been changing slowly as she spoke, a little of the artificial precision and pseudo-refinement chipping away with each sentence to reveal more of the east end Cockney beneath. Now the veneer was almost completely off as she cried, 'I don't want anything to do with murder. I don't want to go to jail. I think I'd die if I went to jail.'

'If you do what I tell you, none of us will go to jail.'

'You killed Bond. And you killed that girl, Anthea Moorhouse, I know you did. Now you're going to kill him. It's got to stop, Paddy, it's got to stop.' She advanced across the room. Hunter waited for the moment when she would obscure Brannigan's view of him. That would be the moment.

But the moment never came. Lightly and gracefully, on his toes like a boxer, the Irishman moved towards her. There was never an instant when the revolver was not pointed in Hunter's direction. When the girl was within a foot of him Brannigan's left hand, clenched into a fist, struck her in the stomach. Then as she doubled over and forward with pain, it came up to strike her under the chin. She gave a moaning cry and fell to the floor.

Pine said something incoherent. Hunter half rose from his chair, then sank back again as he saw the look in Brannigan's eyes. Yet the voice in which the Irishman spoke was soft and calm as ever.

'I'm sorry, kid. But you've got to learn. You can't tell me what I should do or shouldn't do. This is serious. You might be thinking about going to the police. Were you thinking of that, kid?'

The girl lay on the floor sobbing. A trickle of blood ran out of the corner of her mouth.

'Because if you are, forget it. The Bond affair is finished. There was a suicide verdict, you heard it yourself. The police are happy, nobody's going to stir it up again. As for Anthea Moorhouse, this red-headed moron here is the one who killed her. Then he came back here tonight, Arthur became suspicious of him, he attacked Arthur, Arthur shot him in self-defence. You see, I always told you there was some use for Arthur.'

'I don't think I can do it,' Pine said. 'Talk to the police, I mean. Afterwards.'

'If you take a shot beforehand you can talk to anybody.' He spoke again to the girl. 'So you see you've got nothing to be afraid of if you go home and keep your mouth shut. If you don't, you'll be the first one to suffer. Accessory after the fact is what they call it. And when it comes to the point, can you do anything to me, have you got any proof of your story? If you're lucky the police will think you're hysterical. If you're unlucky, you'll be the first one they put away.'

She got up from the floor and wiped away the blood with a tiny handkerchief. 'You've got it all taped, haven't you?'

'Where are you going?'

'Where do you think? Home. Back to the love nest you took for me and never came to.'

'I've told you why I can't come there for a couple of weeks,' Brannigan said patiently. 'It wouldn't be wise. You go home and put something on that face of yours. It's swelling.'

She stood in the doorway looking at Hunter. The blue had come off two of her fingernails. She said nothing.

'And, kid–' Brannigan said gently.

'Yes?'

'If you've got ideas about going to the police and asking them for protection, forget those too. You know me. If you do that, I'll kill you.'

'I know you,' she said dully. One hand was pressed to her stomach. 'I know you now. Don't worry. I'm going home.'

When the outer door closed, the sound seemed decisive. The silence in the room was awe-inspiring, terrible. This is where I am to die, Hunter thought, this is where the world ends, in the room of a drug-addicted athlete I am to be murdered by a ghost from the past I've been running away from. We can never run far enough or fast enough, he said to himself. There's no such thing as a clean break.

There was a slight click as Brannigan again lifted the lid of the record player.

Pine said, in a voice that fluted uncertainly, 'What are you going to do?'

'Jesus, you know what I'm going to do. Get out of the way. Go downstairs. You're more nervous than he is.' He put on the record.

'I've got those double you blues.
One of you is kind and one of you is not.
One of you's cold and one of you's hot.'

Pine began to walk towards the door. If he takes another couple of steps he'll be between us, Hunter thought. Just another couple of steps, that's all.

Pine took the two steps. He was saying something in that uncertain voice about his carpet, his furniture. He stood almost, not quite, between them. Hunter's right hand moved to his hip to get his gun, and at the same moment he rolled sideways out of the chair, pulling it down with a crash almost in front of him.

He was clumsy in getting the gun. Taken by surprise though he was, Brannigan was still too quick for him. At the moment that he fired Pine was still moving, saying something unintelligible. The words, whatever they were, were cut off in a scream, a babbling about God and mother. Pine staggered before he fell, and obscured Brannigan's view of Hunter for three or four more seconds. By the time he had fallen to the ground, Hunter at last had his revolver out.

They must have fired almost at the same moment, but Hunter did not hear Brannigan's shot in the deafening roar of his own. He was conscious of an intense, searing pain in his shoulder, and of Brannigan standing there by the record player, with surprise and pain in his eyes. He squeezed the trigger again. The noise was like thunder in his ears. He had time to think how bad a shot he was and then, to his astonishment, Brannigan crumpled, clutched desperately at the sofa near him for support, and fell forward. Blood came from his mouth. The record was still playing.

'One of you's laughing and singing a song,
And one just doesn't make a sound,

Oh, there's one of you alive and kicking, baby,
And one of you's under the ground.'

I hit him, Hunter thought, I hit him after all. There was a smell of cordite in the air, and somebody was crying like a dog. This crying was the last thing he remembered.

Chapter Thirty-five

'He's coming round,' a voice said. It was a voice he knew, one with disagreeable connotations. He opened his eyes to see, close to his own face, the fresh, eager features of Inspector Crambo. He closed his eyes again, and groaned.

'You're a bit of a hero,' Crambo said. Hunter opened his eyes again in astonishment. 'Do you feel up to telling me what happened?'

'Brannigan was going to shoot me. Pine got in the way. I shot Brannigan.' He struggled up to a sitting position, saw that he was in the bedroom leading off Pine's sitting room, winced with pain.

'He put a bullet through your shoulder. It's not serious. Brannigan and Pine are both dead. You killed Brannigan. Pine died ten minutes after we got here. He told us

Brannigan killed Miss Moorhouse. She's down in the cellar.'

'Yes. They told me. That girl I talked to you about, Tanya Broderick. The one who gave evidence about Bond.'

'Yes?'

'She didn't want to be mixed up with murder. She was here just before the shooting. Brannigan hit her. She'll talk.'

'Good. Let me tell you now how the business about Anthea Moorhouse works out. Brannigan and Pine kidnapped her, killed her, planned to get the money. Actually got fifteen thousand pounds which Moorhouse paid over on our instructions. Notes had been impregnated with a chemical so that they couldn't use them. We've got them back. In a cupboard downstairs.' Crambo's face was solemn as a poker player's. 'We don't usually like people playing Sherlock Holmes, but as I say you're a bit of a hero. That's the way I look at it, the way it works out.' Was there a peculiar emphasis on those last words?

'But–'

Through the open door he could see into the next room. Men were taking flashlight photographs, measuring distances. Flashlight bulbs popped.

'Listen to me and don't interrupt.' Crambo's voice was hard. 'I said, that's the way it works out. Brannigan was an agent for a drug distributing organisation. Pine was working with him. Anthea Moorhouse was one of the distributors. She'd become awkward, was threatening to give the show away. Brannigan and Pine decided she was dangerous, had to be disposed of. They arranged the kidnapping to squeeze money out of Moorhouse as well. When you found out about it, doing your Sherlock Holmes act, they were going to kill you too. Do you agree with that? Have you got any objections?'

A sergeant appeared in the doorway. 'The boys have finished now, Inspector. Anything else?'

'No. I'll be along in five minutes.' Crambo was staring at Hunter. He repeated, 'Any objections?'

'I suppose not,' Hunter said slowly.

'If you have any objections,' Crambo said, looking at his high-polished shoes, 'it might be awkward for everybody. There are questions we should have to ask. About Westmark, for instance. You know Westmark?'

'I've met him.'

'He said at first that you'd been to see him. Later, when he heard that Brannigan was dead, he changed his mind and saw things the way I expected. Then one of my men thought he saw you this evening. Thought he had a bit of a brush with you in fact, outside a pub. You don't remember that, do you?'

'No, I don't remember.'

'Just as well.' Crambo laughed briskly. 'My chap thought the man he saw was carrying a suitcase. The money was found in a suitcase, I think I told you that.'

'You did.'

'But there you are, just a coincidence. That's the way it works out, and it leaves you a bit of a hero. Don't you agree?'

'What?' Hunter said. 'Yes. Oh, yes, I agree.'

'What are you thinking about?'

'Brannigan was only an agent. Behind him–'

'I know who was behind Brannigan. I can't prove it, but I know. He was only a medium-sized fish. We'll land the big one some day. Quite a flair for metaphor I've got, don't you think? Would you call it a metaphor?'

'I suppose so.'

'You're wondering why I'm doing this – adopting this attitude, I suppose an intellectual like yourself might call it.'

'I'm not an intellectual. But, yes, I was wondering.'

'It's the easy way out, that's what you're thinking, old Crambo's chosen the easy way out. But that's not all it is, Hunter. There's a lot I could make stick to you, enough to send you up for years, you know that, don't you?'

'I...'

'All right, don't answer, I don't want you to answer. I don't love you, Hunter, any more than you love me. But why should Moorhouse suffer more than he has done? Who's it going to help if he does? There's a lot that I know and can't easily prove. And if I could prove it, what would be the use? Miss Moorhouse is dead. It won't help anybody to drag her name through the mud. Is that what you want?'

'No.'

'Let lying dogs sleep is what I say. Do you agree with that too?'

'It's not the usual way of putting it.'

'Or you might say, a fool and his paradise are soon parted.' If such a thing had not been impossible, Hunter might have thought that Crambo's bright salesman's gaze held a trace of something like pity. 'You'll have the reporters on your tail tomorrow, but for tonight I've kept them off. There's a car laid on to take you wherever you want to go, and a chap on duty who'll give you a hand. Your wound's strapped up, but tomorrow you ought to see your own doctor, or go to the hospital for treatment.'

'I will. And thank you.'

'I'll leave you with an old Chinese proverb. At the Yard they call this my proverbial mood. Those whose hands are twice as dirty as other people's need to wash twice as often.'

It was not until Crambo had gone that Hunter looked down and saw again the faint yellow stains on his fingers.

Chapter Thirty-six

His shoulder hurt, but he was able to walk up the stairs by himself. 'It's all right,' he said to the detective who was following him, 'I've got a key, I can open the door on my own.'

'Sure you can manage?'

'Quite sure. Good night.'

Anna lay on the sofa asleep, wearing an old dressing gown of his – she had always been too lazy to buy one for herself. Copies of women's magazines were scattered round her, on the floor. The French clock on the mantelpiece said a quarter to twelve. He spoke her name, and she opened her eyes.

'Bill.' She sat up, shaking herself like a dog. The dressing gown fell open. 'I thought you'd gone for good. But what's the matter? You're hurt.'

'It's nothing much,' he said, absurdly heroic. 'I was shot in the shoulder.'

'Why, Bill. Who shot you?'

'A ghost. A shadow out of the past I've been so busy running away from. A gigantic shadow.' He felt weak, and sat down suddenly on the sofa.

'You ought to be in bed.'

He felt wonderfully weary, but he said, 'I've got something to do first. Get my wallet.'

'You're delirious.'

'Get out my wallet, I tell you. I can't use my left arm. Now, you'll find an envelope. Yes, that's the one. With two air tickets in it.'

She looked at them, and then looked at the clock. 'For midnight. To Tangier.'

'I told you I was trying to run away. Give me a box of matches.'

'But Bill – oh, all right. I hope you're not delirious, that's all.' He clumsily struck a match and lit the tickets. They watched them burn to ash. 'That's what it was all about – Westmark and all that?' she asked timidly.

'Yes.'

'And now you've given it up?'

'It was a pipe dream. I thought I was making a break with the past, but it was just a pipe dream. I was running away, but you can never run fast enough to get away from a shadow.'

'So you've come back to me. Well, I'm no pipe dream.' Her eyes strayed towards the box of liqueur chocolates, then she looked guiltily away. 'I still don't understand.'

'That doesn't matter. Anna, let's get married.'

'Married?' She felt his forehead, her face full of concern.

'You know you can get a divorce. Then we'll get married. It's what you want, isn't it? And tomorrow morning I'll ring Charlie and ask about that job.'

'You're running a temperature,' she said decidedly. 'You'd better get to bed.'

'Anna, don't be a fool. I told you, I've been playing round for weeks with a pipe dream. Now I'm trying to face reality, and I need a little help. Don't you understand?'

'Is that what you call getting married to me – facing reality?' She reached over, took one of the liqueur chocolates, and settled at his feet among the women's magazines. With a sigh of contentment she said, 'I never knew reality could be so nice.'

The publishers hope that this book has given you enjoyable reading. Large Print Books are especially designed to be as easy to see and hold as possible. If you wish a complete list of our books please ask at your local library or write directly to:

Dales Large Print Books
Magna House, Long Preston,
Skipton, North Yorkshire.
BD23 4ND